Something Snapped—

Joseph couldn't control himself. He walked toward the man, glaring. "Stupid," he spat at him. "Too stupid to do anything but kill animals more beautiful than you are."

The man took a swing at him, knocking him back against the barn. It was the first time in his life he'd ever been hit by anyone.

Now the man was coming toward him, saying, "I'm sorry, Mister, I shouldn't have lost my temper. But I don't like being called—"

"Stupid!" Joseph finished for him. Then with a strength he didn't know he possessed, he threw the rope over the man's head. After that, it was easy. He simply pulled until the man's eyes began to bulge and his tongue to protrude . . .

Something in the Shadows

Vin Packer

PROLOGUE BOOKS

F + W Media, Inc.

Published in electronic format by
PROLOGUE BOOKS
an imprint of F+W Media, Inc.
10151 Carver Road
Blue Ash, Ohio 45242
www.prologuebooks.com

eISBN 10: 1-4405-3926-X
eISBN 13: 978-1-4405-3926-8
POD ISBN 10: 1-4405-5809-4
POD ISBN 13: 978-1-4405-5809-2

This work has been previously published in print format by Fawcett Publications,
Inc., Greenwich, CT.

Chapter One

Upstairs in his study, Joseph Meaker heard Maggie's voice drown out the others. Weekends, Maggie held court in the living room, over coffee and brandy, after a late dinner. Her audience was always a captive one, since the guests were there for the weekend. Last night had been a two-thirty night, and this one? Joseph Meaker glanced at his watch. Ten-after-one. He was reminded of an old Frost poem which ended: "And miles to go before I sleep." Hours to go—Saturday night Maggie was always in top form.

They had reached an agreement about weekends after the last fight, four or five days ago. Joseph could simply sleep in his study on weekends. Maggie would close the door separating the upstairs from the downstairs. By the time everyone was ready to turn in, Joseph would be asleep, and Maggie would sleep in their bedroom so as not to disturb him. After all, wasn't that the *fair* way, Maggie asked? It was certainly no fault of hers that Joseph did not drink and did not enjoy sitting up and talking. "Chewing the fat," as she put it. Besides, Maggie always added, the move to Pennsylvania had completely inconvenienced her, and all it had done where he was concerned was to make life easier. It was Maggie who had to get up at six every weekday morning, in order to be at her office in New York by ten. It was Maggie who had to watch the weather reports and the road reports and the Trenton train schedules; Maggie, who had to rearrange her entire life so they could rent this farm. *And*—the knife's final thrust—if Maggie did not have friends out for weekends, what the hell kind of a weekend would it be for her? A quiet one, maybe? Joseph Meaker thought of that answer, but said nothing. It would only start her off again on her favourite subject: how *he* lived in a dream world. So they had reached an agreement about weekends, and here it was in effect.

Maggie's shrill laughter startled the cat on Joseph's lap. A Siamese cat named Ishmael, after a favourite opening line of Joseph's. One of his pastimes was recollecting famous opening and closing lines of novels, plays and poems; and his cat's name came from *Moby Dick*. "Call me Ishmael"—and then followed the narrator's description of the "damp, drizzly November in my soul." Often Joseph took down his copy of the novel and read and reread the whole opening paragraph. It was always November in Joseph Meaker's soul, and no way to wander and escape it as Herman Melville's hero had. The cat, then, could do it for him, Ishmael—wanderer. Joseph put his hand out and calmed the creature. Everyone downstairs was laughing now, and Joseph wondered if Ishmael felt more than a disturbance at the noise. Ishmael often slept contentedly through the noise of Joseph's typewriter, the noise of the radio—even the noise of Joseph's and Maggie's arguments; but now the cat's ears twitched nervously, and he switched his position on Joseph's lap, and flagged his tail. Oh, there was more to it than the noise, wasn't there? Something else, even more annoying than noise: a door closed to you. Not just the door separating the downstairs from the upstairs, but the door separating Maggie's kind from Joseph's. The Maggies of the world outnumbered the Josephs, and even if that was not a fact, who would know? If there were a million or more Josephs alone in the night, who would count them? Would one of the Maggies leave the bright room, put down her drink, excuse herself from her friends and go off to make the report on Josephs? No, unlikely. A Joseph doing it was even more unlikely. He would never find his way around the Real World.

"Listen! Hush, I'll read it!" Tom Spencer's voice from downstairs now.

"Yes, read it, Tom!"—Maggie's—"Joseph had them printed in Doylestown."

Joseph Meaker did not have to listen too carefully to know what they were talking about. Maggie always got out one of the signs on weekends, to show guests. Joseph had designed them and had them made up as supplements to the standard NO GUNNING signs required by law to keep hunters off your property. Joseph's signs were just as large as the official ones, and he had gone about his land tacking one over the other, on every tree in sight. It was a sort of postscript to the cold legal wording of the official one, and Joseph was aware that his sign was shamelessly sentimental, but he had always liked the poem; "corn" never really bothered Joseph Meaker if it made the point well.

He heard Tom Spencer reading the de la Mare poem now, imagined Maggie sitting back cupping the brandy snifter with that certain smug smile tipping her lips. Joseph's eccentricities pleased Maggie more often than not; Joseph was her conversation piece.

> *HI!*
> *HI! HANDSOME HUNTING MAN,*
> *FIRE YOUR LITTLE GUN.*
> *BANG! NOW THE ANIMAL*
> *IS DEAD AND DUMB AND DONE,*
> *NEVERMORE TO PEEP AGAIN,*
> *CREEP AGAIN, LEAP AGAIN,*
> *EAT OR DRINK OR SLEEP AGAIN—*
> *OH, WHAT FUN!*

Laughter and squeals and Maggie's voice again above it all, "Isn't it per-fect? Per-fect!"

"Per-fect!" Tom Spencer's.

"Per-fect!" Miriam Spencer's.

Joseph Meaker reached on the table beside him for the package of Flents. From it he took one of the pink wax plugs and popped it into his right ear, then another for the left. The noise became a humming, a buzzing; and he went back to what he was doing: reading over the letters, the poems, the notes—all that was in his Varda file.

"*. . . and my dear, I love your soul—profound, sad, wise and exalted, like a symphony. . . .*"

2

"Don't be silly! He has his Flents in his ears," Maggie Meaker said. "Joseph shuts the world out with wax balls! Ah, but he's sweet! God, but he's sweet!" She was sitting crosslegged on the couch, wearing the new red gondolier's pants from Bonwit's, cradling her brandy in her palm, smoking the new brand of cigarette Albion & Frazier was launching. The confirmation that A. & F. had won the account had come through yesterday; Picks were unfiltered, regular-size cigarettes, and A. & F. was supposed to dream up a campaign which would emphasize the pleasures of the past, the old way of doing things. Tom Spencer and Maggie were to work on it together; Maggie, in charge, of course, because of seniority and experience.

"He really is sweet," Miriam Spencer agreed.

"He must hate advertising people!" said Tom.

"*I'm* advertising people," Maggie laughed. "No, Joseph's just different. A loner, you know? Dreamer. He'd do the same if I had the Queen of England out for a weekend. That's just Joseph."

Maggie reached across for the bottle of Remy Martin and refilled everyone's glass. Her own was full. She was two or three ahead. At A. & F. when men went to lunch with Maggie, they often did not appear in the office again until next day, Maggie always came back, no worse for three or four martinis and a brandy or two after the meal, but Maggie's lunch dates (the men, not the women who never tried keeping up with her) faded off to steam rooms, early trains, or some movie to sleep through. Maggie held her liquor as well as she carried her age. At thirty-eight she had a full figure, not a thin girlish one by any means, but certainly not one that inspired her to read the Metrecal ads all the way to the end either. She was a 36-C with no sag, and a perfect size 14. Her skin was clear and softer than many women's, and her features were good, strongly feminine, in the wide-mouthed, big-eyed, long-legged way, with large hands and feet, as some very beautiful women have, and coal black hair she wore in a semi-short, windblown fashion. If she was not exactly as beautiful as some of the classic examples of women with big feet, she was a very good-looking woman. She had style and confidence, and she was New York to her teeth.

And Joseph? Her opposite. If Joseph was anything to his teeth, he was Joseph. He was not handsome, and if someone who knew him well (whoever that would be) were asked if he were good-looking, that someone (Maggie) would most likely pause a moment and then answer, "Well, yes, *I'd* say he was." There was room for doubt, in other words. He was extremely skinny and long-nosed, with sand-coloured hair that always seemed matted to his head, since he wore a cap most of the time, and he was nearsighted, though he seldom wore his glasses. The result was that Joseph squinted. One of the things about Joseph, one in a thousand, that Maggie never figured out, was the fact that vanity kept him from wearing his glasses. He would just as soon take Maggie out to dinner in a fine restaurant tieless, with egg on his shirt, but he would not appear in public wearing glasses. If he could help it, Joseph would not appear in public, period.

A lot of it Maggie crossed off as the predictable eccentricity of the scholar. A lot of it, as she always framed it in her thoughts, griped her soul! Before she had married Joseph three years ago, she had thought it would be fascinating to be a folklorist's wife. She had imagined quiet evenings before some fireplace, sitting and listening to Joseph explain folk tales, discuss mores, and describe odd and enchanting peoples no one in the world had ever heard of but Joseph. As it turned out, Joseph never discussed his work and he did not enjoy sitting before fireplaces. He spent most of the time up in his study, and before they had moved to Bucks County, when they were still living in New York, he spent his evenings in the local library. Early in their marriage he had made an effort, but it was so obviously an effort—fidgeting at the table after dinner while Maggie had a second cup of coffee, falling asleep in front of guests—that Maggie finally encouraged him to do what he felt like doing, which was spending as much time as possible by himself. Bed was good, bed was very good, but whenever Maggie made a reference to her enjoyment, it seemed to embarrass Joseph. He never liked to talk about it.

There was a plus side, of course, even omitting bed. Joseph was a real individual, not cut out of anyone else's pattern, nor chipped off anyone's block. He was a beautiful artist, whether he simply sketched Maggie while she was cooking dinner or reading, or whether he did a full-scale oil of the house or a view from his study window. Any other man Maggie knew, who had a talent like Joseph's, would be stacking canvases for a show, or never mind that, off in some garret wearing a beret and waiting for the world to recognize him; but Joseph often painted over his very best work, and never dragged a canvas out for anyone to see. Sometimes when Maggie was cleaning up Joseph's study, she would come across a poem scribbled on his yellow scratch pad. Once she had asked him if she could make a copy of one and send it to *The Saturday Review*. Joseph's answer: "What for?"

Then there was the gentleness of Joseph, the nearly self-effacing modesty of her husband. She had never seen him lose his temper, nor make what even came near a harsh statement, and Maggie had often thrown the book at him. In contrast to Maggie's first husband, who drank himself into Roselawn Cemetery before his thirty-third birthday, Joseph was a *Ladies' Home Journal* dream partner.

"What is Joseph working on now?" brought Maggie back from her thoughts; Tom Spencer, apple-faced and boyish ("Gotta have a gimmick, Mag, gotta get a gimmick"—rushing around A. & F., pushing his way up the ladder with calculated sincerity, fighting the good fight for that plot of suburbia at the end of the rainbow), "Another book?"

"We don't know whether it will be a book yet or not," Maggie said. "The Pennsylvanian Society of Folk Mores has given him a grant to study hexerei."

"What-er-eye?"

"You know, hex signs on barns and everything. A form of Pennsylvania-Dutch witchcraft."

Miriam Spencer exclaimed, "I love hex signs on barns!"

The single word "dumb" came to Maggie's mind, but she smiled sweetly at Tom's wife, and for some reason, said she loved hex signs on barns too. Tom Spencer said he had always thought they were very interesting, that someone at the agency ought to work them into an ad some time. Well, Maggie thought as she sipped her brandy, you can take the Chinaman out of China, but you can't take China out of the Chinaman.

"I mean," said Tom Spencer, "I've never seen hex signs in an ad, and I think we could work up something damn good around them."

"I love them on barns," Miriam Spencer repeated. She was trying hard not to yawn.

Joseph had dozed off. In the dream Varda sat beside him on the steps of Jesse Hall, back at the University of Missouri, blonde hair spilling down her back with the sun on it, warm; she was reading the poem she wrote. "It's called *Dear, Joseph*"——smiling up at him on the steps of Jesse Hall, in the years back at the University.

> *Am I dear to you?*
> *I wish I were.*
> *Dear is the held in mind*
>   *in warm rooms of thought*
> *Do I live there?*
> *Do I live at the fireplace of your eyes?*
> *Dear you call me*
> *I wish I knew*
> *Dear is the tear, the wind soft-voiced*
>   *the peaceful word*
> *Is there peace in you?*
> *Is there*

Is there. Is there——is——and the buzzing seemed louder in his ears, slicing into his dream, waking him. He pulled the Flent out of his left ear.

"Is there any reason why you have to sit up with her all night?"

It was Miriam Spencer's voice outside the door of his study, in the hallway by the bathroom. Joseph Meaker glanced at his watch. Six-past-three now.

Tom Spencer was saying, "Keep your voice down, Miriam!"

"Well, is there any reason why you have to sit up with her all night?"

"We're having one last nightcap together, Miriam. Just one!"

"Every time I hear your steps come up the stairs I think you're finally coming to bed, but oh, no, you're just going to the bathroom, then back down to Maggie for another hour!"

"Go back to sleep, Miriam. I told you what it would be

like this weekend. Didn't I? We've got to work out this Picks deal."

"All night?"

"Yes, all night, if it takes all night, dammit!"

There were angry mumblings then, and the sound of the bathroom door shutting, of feet shuffling down the hall towards the guest room. Joseph removed the other Flent and sat up on the studio couch. Ishmael was curled in a ball at the end of the couch, and scattered on the floor beside the couch were pieces from the Varda file. Joseph picked them up and put them back neatly in the Manila file folder.

> *Dear is the shadow, reflection of us*
> *Ours in light, yet also in darkness*
> *Are you going my way?*

He heard the toilet gurgle, then the faucet running. Ishmael stirred, and he leaned across and petted the cat. One day soon he would get another cat, a companion for Ishmael. The name of the second cat was already picked, from another of Melville's novels, *Mardi*. In that novel there was a golden-haired girl and her name was Yillah.

Joseph Meaker whispered to his cat, "Soon I'll get you Yillah."

In college he had memorized a part of that novel: "The thoughts of things broke over me like returning billows on a beach long bared. A rush, a foam of recollections!—Sweet Yillah gone, and I bereaved!"

He heard Tom Spencer stumble out of the bathroom and down the stairs to Maggie. In ten minutes he would go down to the kitchen on the pretence of being hungry. He felt sorry for Miriam Spencer sleeping fitfully in the doublebed in the guest room, waiting; he would do his best to break up Maggie's and Tom's talk, even though it meant he would have to sleep with Maggie and smell the brandy. He hated the smell of liquor on her breath; worse, she snored when she had a lot to drink. On the floor he saw a piece of the Varda file he had neglected to pick up. By sight he knew it was the letter from Gregging, Austria. He would never forget receiving that letter. It had arrived five years after his last letter from Varda. Five years he spent wondering about her: had she married; was she happy back home; and what was home like—Hungary? And he wrote her; but never received an answer for five years. It had arrived a day before he had married Maggie, forwarded from his old address in Washington Heights. Joseph bent over and picked the letter up. Didn't he know it by heart? No, still he reread it.

Dear Joseph,
I know that if this letter reaches you it will be a real miracle, as I only have your address of several years ago, and so much could have happened to change it by now.
But I do feel the urge of letting you know that on December 30 my family and I escaped from Hungary and are now awaiting transportation to Venezuela, where my husband's mother lives. Are you surprised, Joseph? My ideas have changed during the last few years. I have become so disillusioned with that thing falsely called Socialism which I found in Hungary, culminating in the brutal, beastly suppression of the People's Revolution in 1956. I was tired of the whole thing a long time ago (neither my husband nor I ever became party members), but we simply couldn't stand it any longer and didn't want to see our children be brought up in that awful trap. Besides, George took part in the preparation of the revolution and would have been arrested. We crossed the frontier walking for four hours in deep snow, across fields and woods carrying nothing else than our small children in arms. (Aniko is two years old and Katricka is just eight months now) I met my husband at the end of 1953 and married him early next year, romantically, you might say, against my father's will (he's a Protestant). I wanted the children very badly and adore them.
We are living 20 miles from Vienna in a Refugee Home maintained by the American Mennonites. They are such nice people! We have to wait about three more weeks before we'll be taken to Italy and from there to Venezuela, by boat. (But my letters will be forwarded from here.)
Are you in Europe by any chance? Where are you? And

what are you doing? You must be married with children of your own by now.

Can you send some money, a loan? We haven't got a cent, and George has no friends outside of Hungary, other than his mother who will soon assume enough of a burden. I'll give it back to you as soon as I start earning in Venezuela. I hope to teach there.

I thought of you a lot last week while reading an article on Tom Wolfe in an issue of *Life*. It was about his correspondence concerning *Look Homeward, Angel*. I knew you loved Wolfe and his books.

I think, too, of happy days back at the U. of Missouri, sitting on the steps of Jesse Hall, talking, talking, talking, and of things a happily married mother of two children should have long ago forgotten; but in reflection there is only innocence in youth when now, even in my situation, all is so much more glorious than I had imagined. You would like George, Joseph. He is serious like you, a professor of philosophy.

It is a grand feeling to be able to meet people again and to write to people freely again. I hope you will answer soon.

Love,
Varda

Joseph put the letter back in the Manila file with the rest.

After that letter there had been one thanking him for the loan; then one from Venezuela repaying the loan—then, two Christmas cards. On one, a photograph: Varda, the children, the man she had married. Joseph almost had not saved it. He did not like to see the faces of the intruders; what right had they to sit beside her—he, with his arm around her shoulder—claiming her?

Joseph sighed. He slipped the file back behind his books in the bookcase, where he always kept it, and he slid his stockinged feet into his loafers under the couch. Once during the first month of his marriage to Maggie, she had looked across the dinner table at him, an eyebrow raised, her mouth tipped with that quizzical smile.

"Were you ever in love?"

14

"Yes?"
"Were you ever in love?"
"Yes."
"With whom?"
"A Hungarian girl."
"Really?"
"Yes."
"Did you meet her abroad?"
"No. At the University."
"Oh. Puppy love."
"Perhaps."
"Well, did you go to bed with her?"

It had been the reason for their first fight, the fact that Joseph had not answered her.

From time to time Maggie would bring up the subject to irritate him. To keep peace, he had told Maggie her name, but he had not elaborated beyond that. It had nothing to do with Maggie and him, had it?

Joseph tiptoed down the hall outside his study, trying not to disturb Miriam Spencer. He could hear the drone of Maggie's and Tom's voices as he made his way down the stairs, and his hand was just reaching for the door separating the downstairs from the upstairs when he realized Maggie was talking about him.

". . . not like other people, but I knew when I married him he wasn't."

"But you are happy, Maggie, aren't you?"

"Who's happy? I'm cheerful, Tom."

"I never thought of it that way. Sometimes I could break Miriam's neck! She's just not on the *qui vive* about some things! She doesn't get some things! I tried to tell her about A. & F., deciding that most people are really nostalgic for the past, you know?"

"Well, Joseph is. He lives in the past," Maggie said.

"You know what Miriam said to me? 'Tom,' she said, 'do you wish you'd married Irene Littlefield?' Now, honest to God! Irene Littlefield was some dame I was dating way back in *second* year at Cornell!"

"Joseph doesn't talk very much about *his* past, but I know one thing!"

"She didn't even get the point about A. & F. and market research—none of it. She just took it as a personal attack!"

"There's this girl—Varnish or something. Joseph was in love with her."

"I might just as well be an iceman for all Miriam knows about my work!"

"Dear old happy days with Varnish! He's kept all her letters, every last one!"

"Lots of men are married to women who help them. Chris Planter's wife goes to the goddam library and does research for him!"

"I've told him everything about my first husband, but do you think Joseph would tell me anything?"

"Then there's goddam Amos Fenton. God, do I hate Amos Fenton!"

"Not Joseph, he wouldn't—"

Joseph Meaker's hand dropped from the door. He turned around and tiptoed back upstairs.

Chapter Two

"Then why aren't you a vegetarian?" Miriam Spencer wanted to know.

Just as Joseph had anticipated, the burden of entertaining her fell on his shoulders that Sunday morning, while Maggie and Miriam's husband slept it off. He had squeezed orange juice, and scrambled eggs, and now he was sitting at the breakfast table in the kitchen with her, drinking coffee. It was only quarter-past nine; probably no one else would get up before noon, and what on earth would Joseph Meaker do with Miriam Spencer during all that time? A heavy depression began to come in like a slow, smothering fog. To make matters worse, outside it was pouring; they were imprisoned together in the downstairs part of the house.

"If someone doesn't approve of hunting," Miriam Spencer continued, "how can that someone eat meat?"

"I suppose," Joseph said, "because that same someone feels there's a difference between eating what had been killed, and making a sport of the slaughter. I eat meat, but I don't go to Abercrombie & Fitch and buy myself a gun and a special costume for the express purpose of killing what I serve for dinner."

Miriam Spencer said, "I didn't mean to make you angry."

"I don't know where you got the idea I'm angry. Do I look angry?"

"You sound a little angry."

"I don't get angry," Joseph Meaker said. "It never gets you anywhere, does it?"

"It certainly doesn't. I just thought—"

"It's just that next you'll be asking me about my cat," he said. "Of course, Ishmael kills, but it's his nature to hunt."

"Honestly, Mr. Meaker, I wasn't going to say a thing about your cat."

"Oh, that always comes next," Joseph said. "It never fails."

"Well, I just didn't even think about the cat."

"After all, the cat doesn't have any guns or anything. I'd like to see one of these brave hunters catch a rat barehanded! With a rat's teeth on their bare skin?" Joseph gave a snort, "They'd be in some nice shape."

"I like cats myself. I'd even own one, if we didn't have a dog."

"It never fails," said Joseph Meaker. "First people ask you if you're a vegetarian, and then they ask you how come you own a cat."

"Not me, Mr. Meaker."

"Joseph. I don't know why you call me *Mr.* Meaker."

"Joseph, then—I think Siamese cats are absolutely beautiful, I honestly do. They're using them in advertisements more and more, you know."

"I've often wondered what I'd do if one of those hunters killed Ishmael by accident. It could happen, too."

"I bet you'd kill *him*! Wouldn't that be something!"

"I don't believe in killing."

"But I bet you'd be so upset, you'd just—"

Joseph held a hand up. "No. No. I'd never be that upset. No, I don't know what I'd do."

"What would you do?"

"I don't know. I guess I'd try to find out his most vulnerable spot. Then I'd work on that. Find a way to hurt him through that."

"You could hex him, maybe," Miriam Spencer giggled. "Maggie told us you're studying hexerei. You could put a hex on him!"

Joseph forced a thin smile. "Yes."

"I wish you'd tell me about hexes."

"Oh," Joseph said, "it sounds more exciting than it is." He knew what Miriam Spencer imagined she would hear: about demons and witches and spells cast and superstitions, the part that had very little to do with what Joseph was researching.

"Please tell me something about your work," she said. Joseph glanced again at his watch. Nearly nine-thirty. He would have to drive to Doylestown for the Sunday newspaper, but the stand was not open before eleven. Joseph looked across the table at Miriam Spencer, a good look at her; he had not bothered really to see her before now. He saw what he had fully expected to see: a countenance that spelled out for him the certainty that they had not one single thing in common, save for the insurmountable fact that they were prisoners of the downstairs. He did not even dislike Miriam Spencer, which might have helped; he simply felt trapped by his own indifference, and by a monotony that might continue for another three hours. Slowly, Joseph Meaker looked away from that face, turning his eyes to the window and the fields outside, needled by rain, grey, lonely-looking; and slowly he could bring himself to conjure up a different countenance, familiar, unique; and stirring his coffee in an absent-minded gesture, he began to tell Varda about hexerei.

"Hexerei has a tradition that can be traced back to the early Christian arts of the catacombs," he began. "The four- and six- and fourteen-pointed figures hinge around the lily, even the utilization of the lily seed pod is—"

Miriam Spencer leaned forward, practising an expression of absorption.

2

The sun came out in the afternoon, a brisk November wind with it. Maggie took one of the folding summer chairs to the backyard, wrapped up in her heavy car coat, carrying her clipboard and several sharp pencils, a Bloody Mary, and the Picks material. She was going to write a commercial.

Inside the house, Miriam Spencer was spending the afternoon napping over the *Times* fashion ads in the guest room, and Tom Spencer was in and out of the bathroom, vomiting into the toilet. Joseph worked in his study for a while on material relating to European Seventeenth Century tulip symbolism and its connection with the Trinity. Ishmael sat on the file cabinet watching him and purring, and once in the midst of a paragraph Joseph was writing on *sgraffito* ware, he put down his pencil and wondered why he had married Maggie. He did not want to deal with the surface reasons this time (that he had been lonely, that he had found her physically attractive, that they had more or less formed the habit of being together a lot, so why not marry her?). This time he wanted to know,

19

not what was manifest knowledge, but what the motivation was. He had met Maggie the only way a man like Joseph would ever meet a woman like Maggie, by living across the hall from her. Their apartments were the only two on the third floor of the small brownstone on 94th Street, and it was unavoidable that they could meet by the elevator often, ring one another's doorbells during small crises—fuses blown, heat off, a burglary upstairs and ultimately have a drink together. In those days, Joseph still drank. Her stories of the advertising world had amused him in those days, too. They had laughed together a lot, and the first time Joseph had ever made love to her, he had been rather amazed to discover she was not at all sure of herself, but shy somehow, her confidence returning only afterwards, once she had lit a cigarette, brushed her hair back from her face, and sat up. Then she was normal Maggie. It had always annoyed Joseph how she talked about it afterwards, like a football player or a bridge addict, reliving the game in every detail. Joseph told himself his impatience with her at those times was due to the fact he was no longer a young man, and along with middle-age he had acquired the predictable intolerance of others' foibles. But neither was Maggie a young woman, and there was that to tell himself, too.

After Varda, when he had been graduated from the University and gone East to get his doctorate, Joseph had been involved with several women. He had made love with a black-haired girl who had a slight moustache and who never took off her slip—a graduate student studying anthropology. The affair had dragged on for a year; and after her, others. A nurse who roomed near Columbia; a German professor he had met at a faculty party, who always put a stack of marching songs on the phonograph before they took down her Hide-A-Bed; and three or four other women, less easy to distinguish. Suddenly Joseph was thirty-six, and Maggie, across the room from him was saying, "Why don't we give it a try? Lord, as it is, we practically live together."

Had marriage happened to other people in the same random way? Unmarried people at 36, 37, 38, who suddenly leaped headlong into something they somehow had avoided for years, with someone they knew less well than girls they had known ten years ago? Was that moment of their marriage—the moment when it became a fact—the same for them as for Joseph? He had thought of it as being "the hour of lead"; he had read in a poem somewhere about such a moment, "the freezing and the numbness—then the letting go." He had remembered himself a very young man wondering about such a day far off in the future, about his bride, who she would be and what it would be like, and how on earth it would all be accomplished and then happily ever after, and that young man that he had been, broke his heart to remember. Was everyone disillusioned, whether they had married at 21 or 36? Or was it that, for Joseph, disillusionment itself was an illusion?

There were no answers that Sunday afternoon, only the facts, and across from him, the eyes of Ishmael watching him. Pitying him, maybe? Ishmael had known Joseph for ten years. Had he always pitied Joseph?

"You know me," Joseph said to the cat. "Tell me what I'm like."

He reached out and picked up the cat, and held him close to his face. He remembered something Maggie had said once about Joseph caring for no other living creature in the whole world really, but that Siamese cat! To Joseph, it was a fair statement.

3

Maggie had shouted at everyone to come downstairs and hear the commercial. White-faced, trembling while he picked up his cup of coffee from the saucer, Tom Spencer sat in the rocking chair in the living room, his wife on the hassock at his feet. Joseph leaned against the doorway between the living room and the kitchen, and Maggie stood in the centre of the rug.

"Testing, testing—one! two! three!" she said. "Now, no kidding, I want everyone's frank opinion on this, and don't spare the rod. Okay?"

"Go to it!" Tom Spencer said weakly.

"I can't wait," Miriam Spencer said.

Acting out both parts, Maggie read her first Pick commercial.

ANNOUNCER: Ladies and gentleman. Pick cigarettes bring you three minutes of uninterrupted silence. (Momentary pause; then:)
GIRL'S VOICE: (in a whisper) You mean we're not supposed to talk?
ANNOUNCER: (whispering back) Not during a Pick commercial.
GIRL'S VOICE: (whispers all the way through) How can you sell Pick cigarettes if you don't talk about them?
ANNOUNCER: (whispering all the way through, too) The public is tired of noisy commercials. They're irritating. That's why Pick cigarettes have bought silence. Now, shhhhh!
GIRL'S VOICE: You mean you're not going to say anything about Pick cigarettes being unfiltered, and giving the smoker the enjoyment he used to get from cigarettes? Mild, mellow—
ANNOUNCER: Will you please be quiet? People know all that about Picks. People everywhere are picking Picks. We don't need to sell Picks! Shhhhh, now.
GIRL'S VOICE: Gee, Picks taste so good though.
ANNOUNCER: Shhhhh.
GIRL'S VOICE: I love to talk about Picks! It's like reminiscing about the past, about the old days when—
ANNOUNCER: Shhhhh!
GIRL'S VOICE: When cigarettes used to taste this good. When—
ANNOUNCER: Please, you'll irritate the public!
GIRL'S VOICE: I was just going to say, when there weren't commercials irritating the public, those old days; that's what Pick makes me think of!
ANNOUNCER: Will you be quiet please, Miss?
GIRL'S VOICE: Can't I ever say anything? Not even Picks?
ANNOUNCER: Eventually, but not now. Shhhhh.
GIRL'S VOICE: Well, when, for heaven's sake?
ANNOUNCER: Now!
GIRL'S VOICE: (no longer a whisper) Pick Picks!

"Maggie, no kidding, you're colossal!" Tom Spencer
was on his feet, rushing across to congratulate Maggie,
colour coming back to his face, "Colossal!"

"That's the word all right. Colossal!" Miriam Spencer
said.

"Colossal," Joseph said in a dull voice. He had not
meant it to sound dull; he had wanted to go along with
everyone's mood; it had just come out flat.

Maggie said to him, "Thanks for your vote of
confidence, Joseph. I don't know what I'd do without
you." Reaching for her Bloody Mary from the mantle of
the fireplace, "On second thought, I know exactly what
I'd do without you—I'd soar!"

"I wish I could think of things like that to say when
Tom and I are squabbling," said Miriam Spencer.

"You'd better not," her husband told her. He laughed,
crossed over and slapped Joseph on the back. "When I
was a serious young fellow in Cornell, I wanted to be an
anthropologist one year. Maggie ever tell you that? I
wanted to be a scientist, go out in the bush and do
research. I bet Maggie never told you that, Joseph."

"I might have," said Maggie, "if we ever talked together
about anything."

"What changed your mind?" said Joseph.

"Hmmm?" Tom Spencer looked blank.

"About being an anthropologist?"

"Oh *that*! Well, I guess I just grew up. Hell, I don't
mean that the way it sounds. I just mean—well, I changed
my mind. My point was, not everyone in advertising is
stupid. In a way, an ad man has to be something of a
psychologist. Figure out what gets people, you know,
Joseph? Hell, Maggie's ad is a real gas! People'll talk
about it!"

"Yes," Joseph said, "I agree." He did not know why it
was always like this when he was around Maggie's friends;
it was as though they thought he disapproved of them *and*
Maggie, and they were impelled to apologize for
themselves, or defend themselves; and once a rather bull-
faced husband of one of Maggie's old girl friends had
taken Joseph aside and said, "You know, fellow, a lot of
us who are close to Maggie think you're a damn lucky
guy." Joseph could never think of anything to answer at

times like that, but it always set him wondering about friendship. He had never been able to accomplish friendship. Had he ever tried? In college he had lived across the hall from an Indian student, in the boarding house assigned to foreign students and out-of-staters (Joseph was from Vermont) and a few times he had visited the Indian in his room. He was curious about India, and he would ask questions about it, but the Indian was obsessed with America's popular songs, and could talk about little else. "I sing you a new 'pop'," he would grin at Joseph, and then he would keep Joseph there while he went through one after the other, off-key, giggling fitfully at intervals, then launching onto yet another. "I dun vant her, you kin haf her, she doo fat for me, she doo fat for me, she doo fat for—" And Joseph had known a student from Joplin, Missouri whom he had met in his statistics class; they had gone for coffee together from time to time, but the boy stuttered badly and was even less inspired at conversation than Joseph, so that often they sat over their coffee in silence—a silence which was emphasized by the sounds of collegiate congeniality around them. There were other acquaintances, of course, and Joseph often went to dinner at his professors' homes, but he had no knack for intimacy with members of his own sex, nor did he ever think of women as friends. Certainly Varda belonged to no one category like that. One Easter he had coloured a hardboiled egg for her, and in ancient script around it he had lettered VARDA IS! And so she was—the world, perhaps, but not a friend. When Joseph left Missouri to study in the East, and ultimately to teach at a private school in Manhattan and work on various research projects, he found himself even less inclined to meaningless socializing. Often he drank by himself, but he brought that habit to an abrupt halt when he began blacking-out, when there were mornings he awoke with blood on his shirt, or a bruise of some kind on his person; or on the bureau where he left his change, a match folder from a strange bar he could not even remember being in. Those incidents were like nightmares to him, and after one of half a dozen, Joseph gave up alcohol altogether. Within a few months from his swearing-off, he took Maggie up on her proposal of marriage. When Maggie told him it was up to him to produce a best man for the ceremony, Joseph asked his dentist. He had had a great deal of trouble with his teeth the year preceding his marriage, and he had come to know Dr. Saperstein rather well, though they had never once seen one another outside of Saperstein's office. At least, Joseph could think of no one else with whom he had talked so often; so he had put the proposition to Saperstein, adding that he hoped the doctor would not mind giving up a Saturday afternoon for such a purpose. It had surprised Joseph that his dentist had seemed very embarrassed and even slightly irritated, but Saperstein showed up dutifully at four o'clock at the church, and after the ceremony he presented Joseph with a tiny gold stickpin he had made himself, from the gold he used for fillings. It was Joseph's sole wedding gift—the others were all from Maggie's friends, intended for her, but presented to Mr. and Mrs. Joseph Meaker.

Joseph gave up his pointless musing and, bracing himself, walked across the living room to his wife. "I like the commercial," he said. "I never said I didn't like it, did I?"

But Maggie was quick to boil; slow to simmer down. "Why don't you read some of *your* stuff aloud?" she snarled. "Why don't you read that fascinating piece on the lily motif in early Christian art? That'll put some zip into the afternoon!"

Miriam Spencer tried, "It's really quite interesting, I think. Mr. Meaker—Joseph and I, were talking about it earlier at breakfast."

But Tom Spencer was already putting into practice the tactics of the diplomat—a wink for Maggie, a discreet beckon to Miriam. "Ladies and Gentlemen," said he, "The Thomas Arthur Spencers bring you three minutes of uninterrupted peace!"—leading his wife then to the stairs.

"Oh, fat chance!" Maggie said after them.

Chapter Three

"I am perfectly serious, Joseph," Maggie had said, "wild and crazy as it's going to sound. The only way for you to get along with people is to pretend each and every one of them is Ishmael come alive; then simply treat them the way you'd treat the goddam cat, *if it* were human! For *that* matter, just treat them the way you treat the goddam cat right now, every day. Just give people one-eighth the chance you give that cat!"

Joseph was thinking of that as he pulled his Ford Consul away from the Trenton train station. It had been a stiff parting from the Spencers. Maggie had been too angry still, to drive along with Joseph as he delivered her friends to their train, and Miriam and Tom had seemed sullen during the long ride. For some reason—probably because the pockets of his jacket were much too small, and the jacket too new—Joseph had been unable to get his hand out of his pocket in time to take Tom's, extended in a farewell gesture, and Tom had gone off never realizing Joseph's fingers were wiggling frantically to be free from the wool hole. Maggie would have said, "Well, what were you doing with your hands in your pockets anyway, Joseph, at a time like that? Not helping anyone with their luggage, you can bet!"

Miriam Spencer had revealed her pleasure with the weekend in a clumsy slip of speech, just as she was thanking Joseph for everything. "Thanks again, Mr. Meaker, for asking us home—I mean, for asking us to *your* home, Yours and Maggie's, I mean," and her husband had pulled the sleeve of her coat, jerking her out of the embarrassment.

During their quarrel that afternoon, Maggie had said, "Don't worry, everyone knows you're strange. No one comes out here unprepared. They've all heard you're strange."

Joseph headed towards the bridge that crossed to Pennsylvania, thinking it all over in his mind. "A man who likes cats is odd enough already," Maggie had raged on. "Most men like dogs!"

Joseph had said, "That's not necessarily true. T. S. Eliot likes cats. He wrote poems about them; one I remember began 'I have a Grumbie Cat in mind, her name is Jennyanydots—' "

Maggie had begun screaming then, "Who the hell cares about T. S. Eliot, Joseph!" She burst into tears at that point, took two Miltowns, and began the old harangue about having to start analysis again; about calling Dr. Mannerheim the very next morning to see if he had an hour free.

Then the frosting on the cake: Ishmael began to vomit all over the living-room rug. He had been out eating grass again, and picked that unfortunate moment to get rid of it. "Go on, wipe up after him!" Maggie snapped, and Joseph refrained from making any parallel to Tom Spencer's bathroom-dashing most of the afternoon. It was better not to say anything, wasn't it? Better to hold it in. Joseph knew that by the time he got back to the house, Maggie would be over her anger. She would say something about the rough week she had put in (every week *was*); something about the tension resulting from A.&F. getting the Picks account; something too, undoubtedly, about Joseph not being the easiest person in the world to be married to. That was the way those things ended.

As if to mock his thoughts the radio groaned out some new rock 'n roll message about a dance called the Twist; the vocalist grunting in obscene tones that everyone was "twisting" all over the country, "doin' it in St. Louis, doin' it in L.A.—" Impulsively, tiredly, Joseph finished the rhyme in his mind, "Doin' it in New Hope, in old New Hope, P.A." Then he reached out and switched off the radio. Where was joy in it all? In so many of the modern novels Joseph read, love-making was described in a clinical, antiseptical way. Where was joy? In modern novels it was often a memory in the hero's mind, a memory of some flaxen-haired sixteen-year-old with whom the hero had once walked along a river and done nothing more than held hands; but a wife was not joy. A wife was stretch marks in bright sunlight on a once-young body. Joseph always became confused when he wondered about such things: was that the way Life really Was, the way it was with Maggie and him, the way it was in best sellers? Or was there more? Was he no better than a caricature of some fictional character, off in his room rereading Varda's words?

"Dear is the tear, the wind soft-voiced, the peaceful word—"

Did he dream it or was it real? Were we real, or were our dreams real?

At Washington Crossing, Joseph swung onto Route 32 headed for New Hope.

Actually his and Maggie's house was not in New Hope, though his address was New Hope R.D. No. 1. They lived about seven miles from that town, nearer a town named Point Pleasant. The house was an old one made from wood once used for the barges on the canal; there was a huge rundown barn in back, and the property extended for twenty-four acres. It was isolated on a winding back road called Old Ferry; the other houses on the road were more than a mile away from theirs. Guests who did not have cars had to be met in Trenton, New Jersey; and since Maggie seldom ever let a week go by without having guests, Joseph made this trip often—usually with Maggie beside him. Usually with Maggie blabbing away about something or someone at A.&F. Usually with Joseph the only one to wonder at the sights seen along the Delaware; wonder without mentioning it: who were the pair there on the canal's bank building a fire, spreading a blanket for a picnic, that middle-aged couple there? What did they talk about and why had they planned that outing? Why was the man dressed immaculately in a business suit, and the woman dressed in old slacks? Then farther down, a young handsome man (in his twenties?) by himself with a box full of papers, burning them, pushing pieces that fell away from the fire back into its flame, burning each one carefully, alone. What were they? Old letters? A novel given up? Why had he come here to burn them, to a lonely spot by the river? Then kids—a gang of them trooping along in Boy Scouts uniforms, swinging sticks, knapsacks on their backs, and far to the rear, a lone boy, much taller, much thinner slumped over, dragging his feet, a handkerchief wadded in his hand; he was bawling. Why did the others ignore him? What had he done? Was he some idiot, soft in the head, shunned for his abnormality, or was there another reason for this exile? What were the secrets of all those people, and was there any one among them watching Joseph drive the Ford Consul, watching Maggie beside him in the front seat, wondering about them as well? Wanting to know his and Maggie's secrets?

A wind was beginning; with it, a slight fog along the river's edge. Joseph blinked his headlights out of courtesy and safety for oncoming drivers; theirs blinked back at him. It gave him a strange feeling of involvement with the drivers of other cars. Were they all driven by other Josephs on their way back home, alone? Was this the only communication the Josephs in life had? And there was a car now whose driver left his lights to glare in Joseph's face, and Joseph had the absurd thought: not one of us, are you?

At the crossroads outside New Hope, Joseph slowed for the Stop sign. He noticed the bar on the left, its lights out, closed on Sundays for Pennsylvania Blue Laws. Once on his way back from a visit with a student of folklore at Princeton University, Joseph had stopped in the bar to use the Men's. He had ordered a ginger ale, and the men there—farmers, hunters, truckdrivers—had regarded him with a certain icy hostility, as though he were a child molester or some other despicable form of human being. He had never figured out why the whole room had seemed so against him. Because of the ginger ale? Simply because he was a stranger? All conversation seemed to stop, as though he had walked into someone's living room without being invited, and a sudden despair overtook him then, as though he would always be excluded from every group, no matter how low, or how high, or how in-between. What had they done in life to deserve their belong there, and why hadn't Joseph done it? It had made him so nervous that he spilled the ginger ale down the front of his shirt, and he felt that they were all snickering at him as he walked unsurely to the door, that when he got outside, they would all burst into laughter. So what! he told himself, they were a seedy bunch, the lot of them. He had seen their guns—the hunters among them—piled against the wall by the pool table. He imagined them standing around in there swilling whisky and bragging about how many pheasants or rabbits or quail they had "bagged." He imagined them stalking up to their kill after their guns fired, picking up the dead creature oblivious to the last look of life frozen on its dead countenance, oblivious to the fact they had ended the life with a coward's trigger pull; guns against rabbits; a well-aimed bullet against one quick last leap of surprise—and then would they haul the rabbit home, skin it on the back porch, and give their kids the feet for luck? He had thought all that the day he stopped in that bar, and he had hated the men in there; still he had driven away wondering why not even one so much as looked at Joseph with recognition, the impassive uncommitted kind that at least acknowledged his membership in humankind.

Beyond New Hope, nearer Point Pleasant, the fog lifted. Joseph kept close watch for his turn-off, for the hill-road which took him onto Old Ferry Road. In his rearview mirror, the headlights of another car showed. Joseph moved to the right to allow the car to pass, but it stayed behind him. When Joseph took the turn, the car did too. It was a steep hill, and the road was not lighted. The road twisted and turned sharply, and Joseph had to shift to second to make it. At the top of the hill, on Old Ferry, Joseph moved to the right again. Finally, the car passed him. A black Mercedes. Pennsylvania licence—M.D. It reminded Joseph to do something about getting his plates changed and obtaining a Pennsylvania driver's licence. Pennsylvania did not recognize a New York licence, nor any other state's. It had something to do with a personal tragedy in the Governor's life; the Governor had lost a son—something like that; whatever it was, it had resulted in very strict rules. Just as well, Joseph Meaker thought, too many nuts on the highway as it was, and as Joseph thought that, he saw the Mercedes begin to swerve.
The driver was slowing up, weaving from one side of the road to the other. Joseph was not far from the house by then, closer than half a city block, and he was thankful for that. He himself had been drunk behind the wheel once; he had driven miles with one eye closed to focus better, his brains fried in whisky. It had been years ago; he had been returning from a conference at Yale, and he had

been sipping rye from a flask to make the journey less tiresome. He knew how the driver in front of him must feel. It was a fearful sensation—that of realizing you were out of control and there was not a thing you could do about it. Joseph wondered if there were any sensation more fearful.

Slowing his own car to keep from colliding with the Mercedes, Joseph wondered about the driver in front of him. A doctor. That fact made Joseph all the more sympathetic somehow. From the back of his head, the doctor looked like a young man—perhaps a man younger than Joseph, though it was impossible to tell. Why was he drunk? Was he drunk a good percentage of the time, or was he drunk possibly for the first time? Joseph favoured the latter theory; he was a doctor after all, a man who knew better than to let whisky rot his liver; a man of responsibility, tension—was it tension? He was alone. Had he had a quarrel with a girl? His wife even? Had the girl walked out on him, left him at some party where he felt lonely and unwanted? Had he tried to strike up conversations with others there and been ignored? Had he taken another drink and then another to cover his self-consciousness? Was he drunk now because of a situation like that? It struck Joseph that everyone was miserable, whether they drove Fiats or Ford Consuls or Mercedes; everyone wanted a release. In his mind's eye he saw the driver in front of him pulling up to a car lot and saying, "I want to trade this in for a release." The man in the car lot would scratch his head and answer, "Buddy, I never heard of that car? Is it a foreign make?"

Again the black car swerved violently. That's all right, Doctor, Joseph thought; it's all right, Doctor. There are only two of us to know about it, go easy, slow; and Joseph was rooting for the fellow in front of him, praying to God the fellow did not have some bitch for a wife, who would take his head off when he did get where he was go'ng.

EEEEEEE-OWWWWWW, EEEEEEEEEEEEE, OW-WWWWWWWWWWWWW!

Joseph Meaker slammed on his brakes at the noise. At the same time, the Mercedes charged forward in such a fit of speed, the dust was like a fog in the Ford's headlights. Joseph pulled the emergency brake and slipped the car into neutral. He got out, not sure why or what he thought he would find, even though every nerve end ticking inside of him told him what that sound was. He went to the front of the car with his heart hammering, his hands wet in the palms, his throat dry. With the dust clearing now he could see the animal the Mercedes had struck. The elegant Siamese markings were splattered with blood. He fell to his knees, staring helplessly at the mutilated body of the cat, and when he reached his hand out to touch Ishmael, there was a shudder, one, and then another, and the cat's blue eyes seemed to search Joseph's momentarily for some answer as to why—then they were dead eyes.

Joseph toppled from his kneeling position and sat sideways in the road, his hands cupped over his eyes weeping. While he wept, he knew with a sudden knowledge that Ishmael had not been killed by a careless drunk. He remembered how carefully the Benz had taken the steep hill, how straight it had manoeuvered the twists of Old Ferry Road, before it had slowed to swerve, slowed while its headlights had hypnotized Ishmael; then the Benz had chased the creature from side to side until it caught him. Mission accomplished, the black Mercedes had used all its power to get away, the driver, all his sober skill to take the turns of Old Ferry in the escape. And had some sober mind calculated that the licence plates of the Consul were New York ones, that the driver did not live in this area, that therefore it was safe to go ahead with the game?

Weeping aloud now, the lights of his and Maggie's house in the distance, Joseph Meaker picked up Ishmael and held him in his arms, stumbling to his feet, grabbing the car's fender for support, holding on, waiting for the control that would come. But forgiveness would not come with it, nor would resignation. Because when Joseph Meaker had control again, he would think of some way to use it on the man in the Mercedes Benz.

Chapter Four

Every time Lou Hart looked at another car, he was not sorry he had bought his Mercedes Benz.

"It's the sweetest piece around these parts," a mechanic had told him the night before last. "I had to fight with one of the other guys to be the one to drive it back to you, Doc, and that don't happen once a blue moon. A pick-up-and-delivery's usually pain the ass."

Lou Hart had only owned the Benz four months. Monday was a hospital day, so the New Hope Repair Garage had serviced it Sunday. The mechanic who returned the car that evening also presented Lou Hart with a "sweet" bill. One of the hazards of Benz ownership, Hart supposed—the impression that you were rich enough to afford a Benz was taken for granted. The car was a wild extravagance, but there was no way to explain that to a garage man who had come nine miles out of his way at day's end. Particularly when the garage man's car, waiting for him in Lou Hart's driveway, was a '51 Chevy.

That afternoon at the Doylestown Shopping Centre, Lou noticed a Ford Consul, one of the little British numbers. He had passed it driving into Doylestown, and noticed it when suddenly he saw it turn around through his rearview mirror. The driver had quite suddenly reversed his direction; all the way into Doylestown, Lou had seen the car directly behind him. At the parking lot in front of the Acme Supermarket, the car pulled in beside him. Lou Hart was more interested in the car than the owner, but he did get a brief glimpse of the driver. A thin fellow wearing sunglasses and a red-and-black checkered cap.

Hart went first to the drug store, where he left several prescriptions to be filled. The new clerk waited on him, instead of Mr. Blanding, and Lou was glad for that. For business' sake, Blanding always tried to act cordial, but his opinion of Lou invariably registered in the tight lines around his narrow mouth, and in the coldness of his grey eyes. The new clerk seemed to go out of his way to be nice, and Lou wondered if that was just his way, or if perhaps the young man was reacting nervously to gossip he had heard about Lou. Trying to cover it with a steady flow of banal conversation: yes, Doctor, and no, Doctor, and will that be all, Doctor? Yesterday at the Hospital, Dr. Ingram had passed Lou in the hallway near Receiving; he had waved at Lou and then he had said, "Nice to see you, Louis. How are you getting along?" Not, how are you!—but how are you getting along. Little things like that, always. The Fratnik kids who lived across the road from Lou—ten, or eleven now—the other morning when Lou was out painting the mailbox he heard them singing, "Little Brown Jug," hiding behind the yew tree at the edge of Lou's property; ". . . ha, ha, ha, you and me, little brown jug how I love thee!"

After Lou left the drug store, he took a look around the parking lot. His next appointment was at two-fifteen (a sodium psylliate injection for internal haemorrhoids); it was ten-after-one now. There were not many cars, and Hart decided to chance completing the shopping, saving Janice a trip that afternoon. The Ford Consul was still parked next to his car, he noticed, and the fellow in the cap and sunglasses was standing by Lou's Benz. Lou smiled. Everywhere he went people admired the car, even if they did not admire its owner.

In the Acme he bought some Gravy Boat for Janice's dog. He could never think of Stilt as his dog, nor their dog—it was all hers, as far as Lou was concerned. Stilt was a huge, spoiled French sheep dog, with no toilet training at age three, and an overwhelming urge to knock down most people he greeted. Lou always had to turn his back when Janice mixed hot water with Gravy Boat and presented it to the dog. With his back turned, he did not have to watch the spectacle of the dog eating, but he heard it. He knew the number of slurps—exactly seven—and he knew their rhythm. It was slurp-slurp—slurpslurp-slurp—slurp-slurp. In his office last week three such slurps and one crunch sounded the demise of a garter belt with a Gelhorn pessary, made for Mrs. Knappenburger, a farm woman suffering from prolapse. Since then, Lou had often sat around wondering exactly how many slurps could finish him off; put him out of practice altogether. It was a dreary practice anyway, what was left of it. He might well have specialized in proctology, anticipating the ailments he treated these days: hernias, polyps, fistulas, colitis—and he knew the farmers who came to him for treatment, came out of respect for old Lou Hart, Sr., dead six years now, the best general practitioner Bucks County had ever had.

Lou loaded the Acme's wagon up with Gravy Boat and can after can of dog meat, and at the butcher's counter, he picked out a huge bone. With Tony off in Paris, Janice was damn lonely, and if Stilt could fill even a crack of the gap left by their son's absence, Lou Hart could afford to replace a garter belt with a Gelhorn pessary now and then. As nutty as Janice was, she was not a difficult woman and she never had been. She had produced a son for Lou, and certainly the way Tony had turned out could not really be blamed on Janice. A mother may be attached to her boy, may be over-attached, but a mother does not set out to deliberately make him peculiar. Lou Hart realized he had a share in the blame. He supposed he had left the bringing-up of Tony too much in Janice's hands. During the days Tony was growing up, Lou had still envisioned every call, working fourteen and sixteen-hour days, accepting a load of firewood for payment (a mule once, too), and satisfying some naive idealism in himself with the knowledge that he was bringing the most modern Johns Hopkins methods to the backwoods. He and his father had the big Cruller house near Doylestown in those days, and sometimes the only look Lou got at Tony was a glimpse of him through his office window, a small figure wearing a wool stocking cap, playing out back in the sand lot. Tony seemed to grow up overnight; and grown, he seemed awkward around Lou, relieved to have Janice join their conversations. At times Lou felt Janice and Tony left him out of their little inner circle, but, of course, it must have been the other way around. Now, at forty, Lou thought very little about the matters anymore. Perhaps it was he who was relieved now, glad Tony had gone abroad to study. It was less embarrassing that way for both Tony and Lou; neither one had to apologize for the other. Both were what they were.

Now, at forty, Lou Hart was resigned. There were compensations in life, never mind the conditions: Janice and Lou got along well, there was a good deal of love between them, and this year things had seemed to take a turn for the better. Lou no longer kidded himself the way he used to, by telling himself he was going on any permanent wagon—but there were long intervals between the really bad bouts now—and last spring they had bought the house they had always wanted to own—the Clymer place on Old Ferry Road. It had taken every single penny Janice had left from her grandfather's estate; and all of Lou's inheritance. Yet when Lou had mentioned wanting to buy the car, Janice had done nothing to discourage him.

Life was quieting down, Lou felt; it was unsurprising and unheroic, but there were always the compensations. Bucks County was one of them—everything about Bucks, Lou Hart loved. Whether he was driving along the back roads like Burnt House Hill Road, on his way to the hospital in New Hope, or whether he was just driving along plain old Route 611 to do errands in Doylestown, he loved the countryside. Born in Doylestown, he had a country look about him, more indigenous to someone born in the backlands. His face had a certain rustic rawbonedness and a hue to it that gave the impression he had an outdoor job; his hair was straight and blonde, and his features were sharp—a long nose and a pointed chin, with high cheekbones and light brown eyes, a long mouth with narrow lips. His body was not thin, but filled-out and strong, and he had long legs, though he was not really tall, five-foot-eight. He might be mistaken for a farmer, or a truckdriver, or a man who practised a trade of some sort: plumber, roofer. His years at the University of Pennsylvania, then at Johns Hopkins, had never improved his apple-knocking flat "a" tones, and he had that slow, lazy-sounding way of expressing himself that folks from Bucks often have.

Leaving the Acme with his wagon filled with groceries, as he pushed it through the automatic doors, heading for the parking lot, Hart caught a glimpse of himself in the reflection of the glass. Did he look forty? He liked to think he looked far from it, but he remembered that when Tony was in high school, he had always thought that Tony and his classmates appeared much more baby-faced than he and his friends had been at the same age. He supposed one always imagined they looked older when they were

36

younger, and younger when they were older. He wonderd why he cared anymore; after all, surprise was a thing of the past. Wasn't that what made the present bearable now? Life around him was very nearly predictable. The surprises, the unpredictability, was all in the newspapers, was all happening to someone else; why did he care if he looked his age? He had no inclination towards vanity; God knows, not even towards a healthy ego.

When Lou Hart reached his car, he found the same man there—the driver of the Ford Consul. The man was leaning against Lou's Mercedes, the dark glasses hiding his eyes, his arms folded across his chest. Lou pushed his wagon up to the door which the man was leaning on. The man did not move away.

Lou said, "How are you?"

"Fine thanks. This is your car, *isn't* it?"

"Yes."

"It's a very handsome car, isn't it?"

"I think so." Still the man stayed there, with Lou facing him, the wagon between them.

"Tell me," the man said, "do you live around here?"

"About nine miles from here," said Lou. "New Hope R.D. No. 1, but it's closer to Point Pleasant."

It was a cold day for October, and though there was a bright sun, Hart had worn only a wool shirt, and he felt the wind chill his bones. He shifted from one foot to the other, during a pause, while the fellow leaning against his car said nothing. Through the dark glasses, as close as they were to each other now, Hart could see the fellow's eyes. They were watching him, almost as though the fellow were calculating something. Did he want to buy the Mercedes?

Then he spoke, "You don't live on Old Ferry Road by any chance?"

"Yes. Yes, I do. How did you know?" Lou asked.

"I do too."

"Oh? Well. That's quite a coincidence. Where do *you* live?"

"In the big white house," the fellow said; "just as you come around the bend from the steep hill. You know the place?" Still he did not move away from the car door.

"Yes, sure. It used to be the Burgess farm."

"That's the place."

"Yes. Well, we have the Clymer place—look, I have a lot of groceries here, and I'm in a bit of a hurry."

"The Clymer place?" the fellow said.

"About a mile down from you, other side."

"I don't go in that direction much."

"Then you probably don't know it." Lou was growing impatient.

"No."

"Look, I'm sorry, but I have an appointment—"

"You live off the road to Danboro at that end of Old Ferry, hmm?"

"That's right. Yes. Now—"

"You probably drive by my place a lot."

"Maybe every day or two—why? Is there something—?"

The man interrupted him in mid-sentence. "I think I saw your car go by the night before last."

"Possible—why?"

"Is it?" said the fellow. He was watching Hart with those same calculating eyes.

"Yes, sure. Now, if you don't mind, I'm going to load up."

The fellow stepped aside, but he did not go away. Lou Hart opened the door of the Benz, then began lifting the packages from the wagon and putting them on the front seat. The fellow watched him silently. When Hart had finished, he wheeled the wagon back across the parking lot. Hart gave him a perfunctory wave and went around to get into the driver's seat. Settled behind the wheel, he found the man standing by the door of the car, leaning on the window sill, looking in at him.

The fellow said, "My name is Joseph Meaker."

"How do you do? Uh—mine's Lou Hart."

"Doctor Hart?"

"Yes."

The fellow stuck his hand through the window. "How do you do?" he said. He had a firm handshake, one which was somehow intimate, it seemed for he held Lou's hand for some slow seconds before he let it go, and the while he watched him.

Lou said, "Is there something you want?"

"Yes. There is."

"Well, what is it?" By now, Lou Hart's impatience was pronounced in his tone.

"I'm sorry. I didn't mean to make you angry."

"What do you want, Meaker?" Lou Hart said. It was strange, or was it, that the moment he got the words out, Lou Hart saw a sudden scene in his mind's screen. An afternoon in a shop in New Hope, some years back. Lou had gone there to buy Janice a birthday gift. Tony coming along a bit reluctantly. Tony knew the owners of the shop, he had suggested they buy Janice's present there. Lou had been busy looking through their stock when he became aware of Tony's voice, in the rear of the shop. It was the high pitch of anger in Tony's tone that had alerted Lou; and Lou had looked back and seen his son's face red with anger, seen him at that moment give a sudden little stamp with his foot as he addressed the shop's owner.

Joseph Meaker was saying something then, bringing Hart back to the present moment. ". . . to come to dinner," was the end of it.

"I beg your pardon?" Hart said.

"I said, would you like to come to dinner at my place? Friday night."

"Thanks anyway." Hart put his key in the ignition, starting the Mercedes.

"Drinks then? How about drinks?"

With a little self-indulgent irony, Lou Hart said, "I don't drink. Sorry." He released the emergency brake and pulled away. In his rearview mirror he saw the man standing there, watching after the Mercedes, his hands on his hips, the yellow scarf he wore around his neck blowing in the breeze. Lou chuckled to himself, but it was not a very enthusiastic chuckle. *That* sort of thing, for Hart, was always striped with a certain sadness. Too much of the past came back, too many pictures of Tony crying, of Janice crying with him, "You can't help it, Tonio! It's not your fault, baby." Still, Joseph Meaker had not looked at all strange. Midway home, Lou realized the whole thing had been so unnerving that he had forgotten to pick up the prescription at Blanding's.

Chapter Five

At quarter-to-six Wednesday morning the storm began suddenly; water splashed over the earth like another whole world had landed smack in the middle of the watery heavens above; now it was spilling over. Lou was running around the large upstairs bedroom naked, closing windows, long hairy legs and huge toes Janice always made fun of. Or use to. "Dese ain't toes, Lou-zee, dese is fingers. Ummm, kiss zem!" Long time ago.

"God! Coming down!" Lou muttered.

Janice turned over in the bed and blew her nose hard into a Kleenex she pulled from a wad under her pillow. The sound of Stilt's paws on the bare parts of the floor as he crossed the room made her turn back, greet him. "You afraid, baby?"

The big dog wagged his tail and crept over to the bedside.

"Don't like the bad old mean old naughty old storm?"

Lou was scratching a match, a cigarette hanging from his lips, facing the window, staring out.

"Poor Stilt-zun, baby!" She reached down and hugged the dog. "There's nothing to be afraid of," she said. "All the thirsty ground is getting a drink. You *know* how you drink out of the toilet sometimes when you're thirsty? Well, the ground is thirsty now and God's giving it a drink."

"That's right, Stilt," said Lou. "God is up in heaven flushing His almighty toilet."

Janice said, "Are the floors wet?"

"I'll get a sponge from the bathroom. They're not bad."

"Lou?"

"What?" Naked he always looked so vulnerable to her. All she had to do to forgive him times when it was rough, was remember him naked. Poor, skinny.

"Bring some fresh water, hmm?"

He picked up the glass from the bed table and walked towards the bathroom. It had been good last night; it was always very good when Janice rewarded him, and last night she had rewarded him for being nice, finally, about those people the Meakers. At first he had been very angry with her for accepting the invitation; then he had come around and agreed, what would it hurt? Janice had kissed him like she was nineteen again, nipping his cheeks and neck, surprising him.

It had been that way too often to count since she was nineteen, but it had never been as natural after nineteen, and she had always thought of her younger self there in bed with him, as though her older self were sitting in a chair across the room, tiredly waiting for the high-strung girl in bed with Lou to relax, so she could take her place once Lou dropped off to sleep, send the girl back where she came from, the Past.

"Stilt is a booboly-boo," Janice said, hugging the dog. "Stilt is a little butterfly, not a great big old baggy booboly-boo!"

The dog whined at her silly tones and became himself silly, making coy gestures with his paw on the side of the bed, his enormous tongue flagging the air, trying for her hand.

Lou came back into the bedroom wearing his light-blue towel-cloth robe, slippers, the cigarette dangling from his lips, the glass of water in his hands. She knew it irritated him to have Stilt in the bedroom, and almost as if to aggravate him, she continued talking to the dog. "Booby, booby, boo-boo!"—that way, the way Tony loved and Lou hated. Why aggravate good old Lou? No reason. He brought the water dutifully. He said nothing about Stilt, even gave him a pat on the head as he passed him. Still, "Loopty, doopty, boopty, Stoopty-Stilt!" said Janice. Stilt barked, three sharp crashing barks, and jumped full on the bed.

Lou ignored it. "Can you go back to sleep?" he said to her.

"Doubt it."

"Shall I make some coffee?"

"*I* can."

He hated to make coffee. He made no protest at her offer, and sat on the bureau's edge smoking.

Janice pushed the dog off the bed.

"Really coming down!" said Lou.

"I can make instant and bring it up to you right away, or wait twenty minutes for regular," Janice told him.

"All right. Instant."

"I told you I could make regular if you want it!" Janice said. She wondered why she felt mean that morning. It even was in her voice, the meanness.

"Instant is fine," he said.

Janice walked out of the bedroom, "Come on, Stiltsy, Pill-Stilt, *mon* booby!"

"Go on with her," she heard Lou say. "Get the hell—" and a smug smile of satisfaction pressed at her lips over the accomplishment of his anger. She went downstairs wondering why sometimes, for no reason, she played this game with herself; to see if she could ignite his anger, even when she loved him and would do anything in the world for him—except make regular coffee if she could worm out of it.

She boiled the water, listening to him move about upstairs. She heard the sound of the hallway closet opening, being closed—it stuck, so he had to bang it a few times; but it was a gentle bang—over the anger as quickly as she was over her meanness, and she thought, oh God, not the goddam back-number magazines at six in the morning! She measured out teaspoons of coffee. All right, what of it if he killed time that way! Let him read all the old *Looks* and *Lifes* he wanted to, back to the Dark Ages, for all she cared, why should it get her? Then she knew the reason she had felt mean: Lou had just plain out and out stopped caring one so-called tinker's goddam about Right Now. Last night had proved it! They had not had an invitation to anyone's house for dinner since Mother Hart was alive and used to have them on Saturday nights!

Lou had said, "Who the hell meets people by walking up to them in a parking lot and introducing themselves! Then inviting them to dinner!"

"Maybe," Janice had said, "Just maybe, Lou, that is the way it is being done now, for all *we* know. Times may have changed, for all *we* know. All *I* know is that at this point *I* would accept an invitation at dinner at a werewolf's house!"

Janice put sugar in her cup and cream in Lou's; then poured the boiling water into both and stirred. Sure it was strange: guy just marches up to Lou at the shopping centre, introduces himself; next day his wife calls and asks them to dinner. Janice herself would no more do that than ride a horse naked through Philadelphia, but she supposed some people were like that. They were new out here and all; he'd noticed Lou's car passing his house, found out they lived on the same street. What of it? Pssss; Janice chuckled. She had married Lou a year before she was twenty, and her twenties were Lou's head buried in medical books while she turned into the "before" version of a Good Housekeeping Clinic on Young Newlyweds. Lou was like dope or something. She had loved him too much; her mother always told her that and it was the truth. Diapers, dishes, dusty volumes from Father Hart's library stacked on the floor—all in one furnished room and Janice barely out of bobbysocks.

From the shelf beside the stove, Janice grabbed a teakwood tray, set the cups of steaming coffee on it. The pyjamas lent her a younger look than dresses did; they were Lou's, and too big, so they hid the fact she had put on weight, weighed nearly 150, and she was tall, too. Face it, it's fat, she told herself; herself was not too disturbed. She was all right. Red hair and freckles and blue eyes, no more looked thirty-nine than Lou looked Chinese. Tony said she was a dead ringer for Greer Garson, and Tony would sit around with her and talk, tell her all the gossip about the stars! His imitations of Louella Parsons used to leave Janice doubled-up. "And now here's another exclusive from Hollywood's film colony—Rita Maybe has a bad case of hair lice, but her physicians assured me this morning that they will not spread to her fabulous thirty-six-inch bust, known all through Filmland. They are strictly head lice; so, good luck, Rita!"

Stilt goosed Janice with his nose all the way up the stairs, while Janice squealed and the coffee spilled on the tray. In the bedroom, Lou was sitting in the wing chair, a magazine across his lap.

"Look," he said, holding up the magazine for Janice to see the cover. "Mickey Rooney and Judy Garland. 1940."

"*You* look!" she said. "Janice and Lou Hart. Breakfast in the bedroom. 1960." She put the tray on the bed table. "The Present."

"Breakfast?"

“If you’d wanted toast, Lou, you should have said so.”

“I didn’t. They have an article glorifying a weekend in Havana. Mickey Rooney was still making Andy Hardy pictures, for Pete’s sake.”

“One thing I hate about this rain is that I was going to New Hope to hunt for a dress this afternoon.”

“What for?”

“For a dress.”

“I know, but what for?”

“I need one.”

“*I* know what for,” said Lou, reaching across for the coffee, “for Friday.”

“All right, for Friday. What’s wrong with that?”

“They could be nudists, for all we know about them.”

“Well, was he wearing clothes at the shopping centre?”

“You never told me exactly what she said when she called. What did she say, exactly?”

“She said she was Mrs. Joseph Meaker. Margie or Maggie, she said, was her first name. She said her husband had told her we were neighbours, and she wondered if we would have dinner with them Friday.”

“And that was all.”

“She said they were both communists and the last time they had made love was two weeks ago, and they had one child who was a hydrocephalic, and one who was a cretin, and neither of them liked prunes, and both were from Tanganyika, and both smoked Newport cigarettes because they liked that cool menthol flavour.”

“Thanks.”

“Well, what was she supposed to say?”

“Who are they? She could tell us that! What do they do? What do they want from us?”

“They want to poison us.”

“That wouldn’t surprise me.”

“They’ve seen that flashy car of yours and they think we’re millionaires. They’re after our money.”

“What did she sound like?”

“She spoke in a Tanganyikan dialect. It was hard to tell.”

“I just hope you think it’s this amusing Friday night.”

“Anything for a change, as the flat tyre said to the jack.”

"I know," Lou said.

She wished he had not said it in such a gentle way, edged with a certain self-deprecation. It made her sorry for him that he was sorry for her, or for them—whichever way it was—and ready to take the blame. She had been enjoying herself up to that moment, sparring with him, pleased by her own sharp humour; she did not like it that he brought her back from there to here, with two words and the old tone of disenchantment. She looked across at him and for the briefest moment their eyes met, and she wished there were a way for her to tell him that half of her was just an act, that none of it had really been that bad. They used to talk and talk, remember? When they were first married they used to lie in bed and talk sometimes until it was light, and neither one had any sleep, and Lou had his classes and she had the mess of the day and Tony already stirring in his crib, but God it was glorious how they never got tired of one another's voice! Even now, she liked talking with Lou; they talked a lot—that was all there was to do—but it was different. Then she used to be able to say things she was thinking. If now was then she could simply have said, "Dammit, Lou, I've liked it, really; it's been good, and I don't *mean* this—the way I am!" But it would just embarrass both of them now, and Lou would probably end it by saying something like, "Well then, let's not go Friday night." It was different. That was why she was always sitting in the chair across the room those nights, waiting for the high-strung girl in bed with Lou to relax, so she could get some sleep.

"Where's dat great big butterfly doggie-bob?" Janice called out. It was as though she was seeing herself as some character in a movie, some woman who was really insensitive, really dumb! Calling her dog the one way Lou hated (was it because she used to talk to *him* that way? Bright gal, she thought, very good at snappy deductions!) while Lou sat there, feeling sorry about everything. She thought, well, say something to him; that lousy "I know" is still hanging in the air above us; so say something.

"You're thin, Lou. I wish you'd eat more."

"Maybe the Meakers will serve up a Tanganyikan boar." He was smiling. He was trying too, she realized.

"I remember the old Andy Hardy pictures," she said.

Chapter Six

Dr. Hart's voice drifted into the kitchen, where Maggie stood poking the potatoes with a fork.

". . . yes, sure, but the symbols differ with the county. There's the star motive in Berks County, and the flower pattern favoured by the farmers around Lehigh and Northampton. I've seen horses' heads, and the iron cross of Germany."

"I've seen the swastika effect in fractur painting," Joseph said, "but never as hexerei. Nor the cross."

"Hexerei plays only the slightest part in the symbols, Joe," Dr. Hart answered, "you admitted that earlier when—"

Maggie smiled at the "Joe." No one ever thought to call Joseph that, and the first time the doctor had said it, Maggie had expected Joseph to correct him. Joseph had done no such thing; in fact Joseph was not himself this evening. He was behaving as though he had had a drink, which he had not had; he was loose, somehow, and very nearly gay. The evening was off to a start very unlike Maggie's week-long, worried conception of it. A moment before the Harts had pulled in the drive, Joseph had said, "Well, it's almost time for Ishmael's killer to arrive." And Maggie had told him again that the whole idea of the evening was the most insane she ever heard.

"That's just what it isn't," Joseph said. "I'm not going to say one thing about Ishmael, not one thing. You'll see."

"What will I see?" Maggie really wanted to know; what was Joseph's point?

Joseph said, "I just want to know what a killer is like. It's only for my own satisfaction."

When Joseph first announced she was to invite the Harts to dinner, Maggie refused to believe he was serious. She made all the predictable protests, such as her thinking they would be the last people Joseph would want in his home, and her thinking Joseph was having a delayed reaction to his pet's death that was not far from the "bughouse," and her thinking Joseph had something else up his sleeve he was not telling her.

But Joseph was adamant. "Just do it," was his answer, "just phone them and stop trying to make a Freudian case history out of it."

It was an embarrassing thing to have to do—invite perfect strangers to dinner; but Joseph had persisted until he wore her down. The next day at A.&F. Maggie was a wreck thinking about it. Tom Spencer said Joseph's behaviour was the typical scholar's.

"Don't you see, doll," said Tom Spencer, "he's got to rationalize his grief, nail it down, understand it. He'll have these characters to dinner and he'll find a way to pity them; then he'll forgive them. It's the old 'understand your enemy' bit."

Maggie shut the oven door and turned the dial to 250. From the sound of things in the living room, Joseph's little scheme was backfiring. He was actually having the time of his life. Maggie herself was enjoying the Harts. She poked her head around the corner of the kitchenway and caught Janice Hart's eye beckoning her.

"Can I help you, Maggie?"

"How many drinks does the doctor like before dinner? Potatoes are done; I can put the steaks in any time."

"Leave it up to *him*, we'll never eat!" said Janice. Maggie and she laughed like conspirators in the grim game of husband management.

Maggie said, "One last one?"

"I'll make it. I'll get his glass."

"Wait, how's he like his steaks? I've got individuals."

"Bloody!" Janice said, making a face. "Medium for me."

Maggie hauled the steaks out of the refrigerator while Janice went for the doctor's glass. From the sound of things, the doctor drank. He was probably drunk Sunday night, never mind Joseph's diatribe about sober, purposeful murder. Joseph was in no mental shape to size up anything or anyone Sunday night. He had cried like a kid; he had insisted on digging a hole out in back, in the dark, burying the cat immediately, and he had sat up past midnight making a marker out of the side of a beer case. R.I.P. he had printed across it in blue paint; "You know what it stands for, Maggie?"

"Latin for rest in peace, isn't it?"

Joseph had said, "No. English for Retaliation Is Promised." That was Joseph's mental shape Sunday night.

Janice Hart put her husband's glass on the sideboard and said, "You think they'd known each other all their lives."

"Wouldn't you? I've never seen Joseph take to anyone so fast."

"Lou doesn't usually take to anyone, period."

"That's odd. I was going to say the exact words about Joseph."

"Really?"

"Honey," Maggie said, "he's not even that friendly with me!"

Janice Hart laughed, and it was understood between her and Maggie how much they enjoyed one another. It gave Janice courage to say, "Lord, and you don't know how I dreaded this evening!"

"Do *you* know," said Maggie, "that Joseph had to practically twist my arm to get me to make the phone call? I said, 'Good God, they'll think we're pushy New York Jews, or something, asking strangers to dinner'." She had said no such thing.

"Oh, it wasn't that you called up out of the blue," said Janice. "It was just that I thought Lou would be bored—he's so unsocial—then he'd blame it on me, and we'd be off to the races, if you know what I mean."

"Janice, my new friend," Maggie said, her Scotches resting warmly inside her, "I know exactly what you mean!"

"Isn't this wonderful?"

"Wonderful!"

"Lord, I think I'll have a third martini. I *never* do!"

"Take the doctor his drink," Maggie said, "I'll make one for you."

"Be right back!" Janice Hart promised emphatically.

Happily, Maggie reached for the gin bottle. She found herself singing a bit of the new Picks commercial, "It's like the old days, sunrays, blue-sky-high-days. Pick a pack of tickled-pin Picks, let go, let go!"

Lou Hart knew he was doing all the talking at dinner, but it was different, wasn't it, when the person listening to you was really fascinated with what you were saying? Never mind Janice and Maggie Meaker—they were high and silly now; but Joseph Meaker was cold sober, his eyes watching Lou's every time Lou looked across the table at him, his head nodding with interest. "Go on," he'd say, "this is interesting to me, go on—"

Lou continued, "Well, I'd heard a lot about these fellows. They're competition after all. Be surprised how many people still go to them too. I thought I'd have some fun, see for myself; so I went to one."

"Isn't it illegal?" Maggie Meaker interrupted. Lou wished the women would take their coffee and go into the living room and chatter, the way they had in the kitchen before dinner. He could reach Joseph Meaker; Meaker was a serious student, every bit as fascinated by Dutch Pennsylvania as Lou was—but Maggie and Janice were just polite, asking needless questions, making idle comments.

"Yes, of course, but so is fortune telling, and all the rest of it. Besides, the police never get any complaints. A lot of these pow-wow fellows actually *do* relieve ailments, same way medicine men are often effective in tribal areas."

"Go on," said Joseph Meaker.

"Tell about that word people say when they think they've been hexed, Lou. What is it? German sounding."

"I will!" said Lou angrily. "If you give me a chance!"

"Oh, my, aren't we sensitive tonight," from Janice; and Maggie giggling over the remark with her. Lou ignored them. He saw the slight flicker of irritation in Joseph's eyes, too.

He directed his conversation to Joe, "*Verhext* is the word. People go to these pow-wow fellows and tell them they're *verhext*, and ask the fellows to help them. Fellow I went to thought I had kidney trouble. You know what he gave me? A sheet of paper. On it there were eight identical groups of cryptic letters, arranged in a square. He told me to cut off a letter a day and eat it. Chew it up and swallow it!"

"God!" Maggie Meaker said. "What a commercial you could write around that product. Friends," she said, imitating an announcer's voice, "have you had your morning paper?"

Janice guffawed, and Maggie shook with laughter, while Joseph Meaker sat stirring his coffee with a glum expression. Lou attempted a smile, since it had been Maggie Meaker's joke, and not Janice's, but he felt the same way Joe did. Why did women have to make something silly out of everything? Particularly when they had a few drinks. Lou Hart had no patience with happy drunks; even common sense said liquor was a depressant.

"Do you believe everything you eat in your evening paper?" Janice trying to top Maggie; both on a laughing jag now.

"Oh Lord," Janice sighed, wiping the tears from her eyes. "Lord, Tony would love you, Maggie!"

"Who?"

"My son. Tony."

"I didn't know you had children!"

"Just Tony. He's on an art scholarship in Paris. He has the same sense of humour we have!"

"You got a grown son? I don't believe it!"

Joseph Meaker sighed, and Lou saw his wife give him a dirty look. He said to Joe, "Why don't we do the male thing, and leave the ladies with the dishes?"

"Fine!" said Joseph Meaker.

The pair got up from the long oak table, before the fireplace in the dining section of the kitchen, and walked into the living room. Lou Hart was high enough not to care whether or not it was proper to bring along the bottle of brandy with his glass.

Janice hissed at him, "Just go easy on that stuff!"

3

Upstairs Maggie was taking Janice Hart on a tour of the house. Joseph hoped they would take a long time; he had been waiting for this moment all evening. Across from him, Louis Hart sat glassy-eyed and confidential, spilling a little of the brandy's ember juice on the marble-top coffee table as he poured more into his glass.

". . . don't know what you're getting at," he was saying. "Sure, a doctor's life is different from other people's; so's a plumber's."

Joseph said, "I mean, a doctor gets a different viewpoint, doesn't he? People are so much flesh and bones."

"So much piles and prolapses!" Lou Hart snickered. "Hell, Joe, these people I treat—these farm people —everything wrong with them's wrong below the belt. I've become a goddam ass doctor's all."

"That's what I mean, Louis. You get a different outlook as a doctor. Life is cheap, hmmm?"

"I suppose it is."

Joseph Meaker watched him brush the pool of spilled brandy with his fingers, wipe them across his pants, sloppy, careless. He thought of Ishmael, how he used to wash his face by licking his paws and brushing one paw up past his ears and around his whiskers, meticulous about keeping clean. Grief tugged at Joseph; he remembered what it was like to leave Maggie and her guests downstairs and go up into his study, Ishmael tagging along at his heels. He felt a crazy urge to blurt out, "You killed my cat and I'm going to get even with you," but he simply smiled at Hart across the table, as though there were nothing in the world wrong. He would get to know Louis Hart and find his own way of retaliating, custom-made for Dr. Louis Hart. He decided it was either going to be a very simple accomplishment, or one almost too complicated to fathom. He liked to imagine that he was enjoying the suspense in the situation, that he was effecting a slow and somehow graceful manoeuvering; but he was well aware of the fact that his emotions were too often taut in the confrontation with Louis Hart, and under the façade of calm there was turmoil. Earlier at dinner, Joseph had looked across at Hart's plate and seen there a piece of bloody-looking animal, done as the doctor had prescribed, and the steak in Joseph's mouth, cooked well-done, with not even a pink shade to it, had tasted sanguineous suddenly; horrible! He had wanted to shout, "Get your blood-lust out of my sight; you, go!" But instead, he

covered his own steak with a leaf from the salad, unable
to eat any more.

"I still don't get what you mean?" Hart said to him
now.

"What I mean, is that seeing death is sort of a part of
your business. The body is dead; long live the body. Do
you understand me?"

"Yes. Death doesn't mean much."

"Did you ever think that a doctor makes a perfectly
understandable murderer."

He saw Hart hesitate, saw Hart's face blanch. "No."

"Well, think a moment, Louis. Look at the big murder
cases. Dr. Sam Sheppard. Dr. Adams. Dr. Finch. Always
doctors. Why? Because they see death all around them:
they know better than anyone that life amounts to a bag of
bones. It's easy for them to murder."

"Just the opposite, I'd say. It's hard for anyone to
imagine someone who saves lives, taking lives. So it makes
better newspaper copy!"

"Still where are the famous murder cases involving
lawyers, or clergymen, or professors, or bankers, writers,
artists?"

"I don't follow murder cases. I don't know. Why do
you know so much about it all, Joe? Whatsa folklorist
doing reading murder cases?"

"The newspapers are full of them!"

"Who played the world series this year, Joe?"

"How would *I* know?"

"Newspapers are full of sports, too."

"Look," Joseph Meaker said, "*I* haven't got anything to
keep *me* awake nights."

"Ha! I wish I didn't."

"Ah, so you do, hmm?"

"What are you getting at?"

"Let me put it another way," said Joseph. "What do
you think of hunters?"

"I don't think about them."

"Do you post your land?"

"Sure. Little enough business without them knocking
off a good case of gastrogenous diarrhoea on me!" Lou
Hart chuckled and reached again for the brandy.

"What's your philosophy about hunting?"

"Well, I only know about the deer. This is a surplus area. I've seen them come into my place starved. A bullet in the fall is kinder than slow starvation in the winter."

"Do you think the hunters are hunting out of kindness, Louis?"

"Naturally not. But the result's the same."

Joseph had felt so near a short time ago; now it was slipping, the moment was passing, like dreams, when the thing you are trying to catch hold of escapes through your fingers, swift slippery.

Louis put the cap back on the bottle of Remy Martin. "We're all of us hunters in a way?"

"How do you mean that? I'm certainly not. I've never hunted anything."

"You never squashed a mosquito with your hand in the summer? G'wan!"

"All right! If it attacked me, I defended myself. But Louis, I have never in my life bought a special instrument with which to kill a living thing! Never! Not even a mousetrap!"

Louis was laughing at him suddenly. Joseph resented it, interrupted it with a protest, unexpectedly loud in its tone, "I haven't! I never have!"

"Aw, Joe! You're going to lose this argument, I'm afraid."

"Oh, no. No, Louis. I'm speaking the truth."

"Joe, there's a fly-swatter hanging out there in the kitchen. Did you ever use it?"

Joseph Meaker's face was as warm and stung as though he had been slapped hard by this man; he could feel himself blush, feel the shortness of breath in him while he searched for an answer. Louis was laughing again. "Life is life, Joe boy. You're not a God. You hunt flies with special equipment; the hunter goes after a deer with a gun. Did the fly have any more chance than the deer? Or is our argument really about what life is valuable and what life isn't? That's a moral question, a philosophical question. No, Joe, I have you!"

Joseph Meaker was on his feet now, shouting out his retort, pointing his finger at Louis Hart, "And a cat's life, Louis? A cat's life?"

"A cat's life, a dog's life, a deer's life, an ant's life, or the life of a bacterium—any life! Is it up to you to say which is more valuable, Joe?"

"I'm talking about the pleasure in killing!" Joseph shouted. "I'm talking about the deliberation, the certain feeling or sensation of power! *You* know what I'm talking about!"

Louis looked up at him with a smile, a playful one which Joseph wanted to wipe from his mouth with the palm of his hand. Louis said, "Are you talking about the satisfaction you get when you've nailed one of those goddam pesty flies with your swatter?"

But Joseph stood there looking at Hart suddenly without seeing him, his eyes given to the stare of a trance which involved him in time past, and not this moment; and Joseph found himself remembering an afternoon months ago, during the first days in the house. He and Maggie had hung up flypaper. There were countless flies all through the house, for Joseph left the screen door open in the beginning, to encourage Ishmael to come and go freely. That afternoon Joseph had gone into the kitchen for a glass of water, when he saw one of the flies wiggling, stuck hard to the paper, his four legs kicking to be loose. Joseph had gone across to get him loose, but when he tried, he had succeeded only in tearing the wing from the creature, and the moment he did it, Maggie had come up behind him, and she had said, "Oh, pulling wings off flies, hah?" and laughed. Something had exploded inside Joseph then, blown his control to bits, and like someone insane, he had yanked the pieces of flypaper from the ceiling, his hands tangling in their sticky glue, until it was almost as though he were handcuffed by them, and a panic started in him which made him run first to the sink to try and wet his hands free, then the stove, as though he would burn the gummy shackles off. Finally, he headed out the door to the lawn, where he buried his hands in the grass, but only more dirt and some bugs from the earth stuck to the paper, and in that brief instant of frustration, he had felt mad, trapped, the same as any madman in a strait jacket. When Maggie came out after him, she was nearly hilarious; it had become, since then, one of her favourite stories, to tell of the time she had cut Joseph free of flypaper with scissors and a hot dishrag. ". . . and to see the expression on his face!" was the way the story always ended. Whenever she told the story, Joseph's hands would itch; he would begin to feel all through him the horrible sensation of sticky death on his flesh, sticky death hanging on to him, making him its prisoner; flies he had trapped, trapping him.

"Ah, Joe," Louis Hart was saying now, "don't you see? We're never so guilty as when we're innocent."

Then there was the sound of Maggie's and Janice's high heels on the wooden stairs leading from the upstairs—and Maggie's voice, "Do you know we're a lot alike?" Janice Hart answered, "We could be sisters!"

Louis Hart grinned at Joseph. "They *are* alike too," he said. "I suppose *we* must be; after all, we picked 'em."

Chapter Seven

In the two weeks that followed that Friday evening, Lou Hart began to think Janice was right. Joseph Meaker probably *had* heard about him; probably that was the whole point of that dinner: Joseph Meaker wanted a good look at a doctor who was the next thing to a murderer. That kind of gossip could come from anyone in the county, not even a particularly malicious source, either. It was a natural enough thing, wasn't it, to discuss doctors with newcomers; tell them where the nearest one lived, what he was like, fill them in on the matter for their own safety? Could have been a milkman who told him, or Teller, the local fuel-oil supplier; Overholt, who ran the grocery in Point Pleasant, or Harry, the Sunny Beverage Company driver. Anyone, who did it matter? Anyone could have said, "Well, now, you *do* have a doctor close by, but around here we don't take much stock in him."

Then it would come out—all about old Mrs. Tondley calling Lou up seven-thirty at night. Her nephew home on leave from the Marines had been helping out on the farm; his arm got caught in the blade of an electric saw; bleeding badly, and Mrs. Tondley did not drive a car. Dr. Hart said he would be there immediately.

Six hours later Freddy Tondley, who had faced the last-ditch fighting for the city of Taejon in Korea, and the Iwo Jima invasion in the war before that, was dead from blood loss; and seven hours later his old aunt had heart failure because of the shock, but it was a good three hours after all of that when the State Police woke Dr. Hart up on the Mechanicsville road. His car was pointed in the direction of the Tondley farm, but he could not even remember taking the call. Red-eyed, still reeking of rum, he was taken to the Doylestown Police Station. Only luck, translated as lack of sufficient evidence, and love folks in Bucks County felt for Doc Hart, Sr., let him off with a fine, a judge's lecture, and suspended disciplinary action from the State Medical Licensing Society. But no amount of luck or reverence for his father's memory could win back what little confidence there had ever been in Dr. Louis Hart, Jr.

He was always a drinker, and no one ever said any differently, but after the Tondley incident, folks no longer overlooked it; in fact, they rarely saw anything else when they saw Lou Hart passing. Was he walking straight? Circles under his eyes? Did anyone get a whiff of his breath; smell anything? Five years and it was still going on. So was the doctor still going on drinking, wasn't he?

Except for those mavericks who never *would* go along with the consensus, and making allowances for new folks who didn't know any better, and folks who knew he was cheaper than his colleagues (had to be if he wanted business), he was not a very busy man any more. The New Hope Hospital wasn't proud; they let him take charity cases during the week, looking him over good to insure his sobriety when he arrived mornings. He did have a steady trickle of patients, but no where near enough to warrant buying a Benz. That took gall, too; flashing around that way; not many were able to resist a certain sarcasm when they saw him. "Well, *there's* the doctor, if you please, *some* nerve, *I'd* say!" And some, "I hope he's happy with his fancy car! I just hope he's happy!"

Lou knew how people talked. Still, it had never occurred to him that that might have prompted Joseph Meaker's invitation, not until Janice and he were driving home afterwards. There was that awkward moment near the end of the evening when Lou had made the pointless remark about being like Joe, because their wives were alike. Suddenly Joe had grabbed Lou's lapels, leaned towards him with his face only inches away, and then nearly hissed his words, "You think that do you? You think so, do you?"

And even Maggie had exclaimed, "Jo-seph! What on earth—" and had come across and pulled him away from Lou. Somebody—Lou couldn't remember who—made a joke somehow; a take-off on some commercial about tension pounding away, and everyone had laughed, Joseph Meaker joining in. But there was a certain paleness to his face, a certain lack of conviction in his eyes, his stance, in the way he held one hand tightly with the other. Spooky,

Janice had called the moment; plain spooky.

That night in bed they had gone over it for hours. Lou had remembered the discussion with Joe on doctors who murdered, and that had clinched it for Janice. The whole thing, she said, was obvious; then both had stayed awake smoking cigarettes and trying to figure out why it was so important to Meaker. There were all sorts of theories between them. Had he been an old Marine buddy of Tondley's, bent on some subtle revenge? Was he really a folklorist studying hexerei, or was he some sort of popular psychologist doing some kind of research, or a novelist, even? What? Was his wife in on the scheme too, whatever it was? Janice could not believe that Maggie would have anything to do with any scheme.

Still, it was weird, made even more weird when a week later Maggie called Janice for a shopping trip in Frenchtown. The pair spent a very gay four hours with no mention of either Joseph or Lou. The Saturday following—another jaunt together—to an auction up near Carversville. Again, no particular mention of their husbands. Janice steered away from the subject, too delighted with the new friendship to take any chances, and Maggie seemed oblivious to schemes of any kind. Yet Janice reported that once, when she made a casual suggestion that all four have dinner at the Hart's one night, Maggie answered, "It's like pulling teeth to get Joseph anywhere, so don't count on it."

None of it made any sense to Lou as he mulled it over in his mind. In between a Mercury Sulfide tattooing for pruritus and a check-up for a young granite worker, Lou gave it a lot of thought. He was still so steeped in the mystery, that for the first few minutes of his examination of the granite worker, he did not get what the fellow was trying to tell him. Something about needing the check-up because of a certain worry, something about losing something. Lou realized what the fellow was saying when he finally became more direct.

"You see," he told Lou, "I'm Platonic now, and it's getting my wife down. I been Platonic a month."

Lou leaned back in his swivel chair and lit a cigarette. "Where do you fellows get that word? I heard it a lot out

58

here. I've lived here all my life, but I don't remember it being a local expression."

"The fellow writes the column for the *Intelligencer* uses it. You know, the doctor? Writes on health. Well, I read it there, but I never figured I'd get that way."

"I don't want you to worry about it," Lou told him. "We'll give you a good check-over and——"

The fellow interrupted him. "I was never once Platonic before this, Doc! There's got to be something wrong."

"Okay, we'll look you over, but it's not uncommon, Highsmith. It can happen to the best."

"I knew *you'd* understand, Doc. I'd be embarrassed to tell a regular doctor, but I figured I could tell someone like you."

Lou Hart never got used to it; he could feel the warmth of his cheeks, spreading to his neck, ears, and the patient saw his embarrassment, tried to undo it, "You know, Doc, I mean you've had your troubles too. That's all I meant."

"I know," Lou Hart said. He glanced away from the fellow's apologetic expression, distracting himself by looking out the window, mechanically telling the fellow to strip to his underwear. It was at that instant he saw the Ford Consul come slowly down the drive, saw Joseph Meaker behind the wheel.

2

The dreams, of course, were the least of it. Some of them were even rather pleasant, though when Joseph Meaker woke from them, the loss of the cat felt even more terrible to him. But in the dreams there seemed to be neither great sadness nor great exaltation. They were peculiar dreams. In one, Joseph would be opening a can of mackerel, Ishmael rubbing back and forth against his ankles, the way the cat used to do. In another, Joseph would be empying the red plastic pan of kitty litter down the toilet, then lifting the large orange bag over the pan, and pouring in the new litter, turning his head slightly away from the litter's dust, as he used to. The dreams always seemed to remember the commonplace; unlike some dreams, they had neither beginning nor any conclusion, and no point, really; they were like snapshots of a time past. Still, there

59

they were in Joseph's head, night after night, and some afternoon, when Joseph would drop off while he was reading, a minute, two or three minutes, it was hard to tell, but each time—the dream of Ishmael. The dreams, he could have stood; that much was predictable about loss, wasn't it, that dreams would bleed the experience until there was no more life left in the unconscious either; then the loss would be accepted. No, it was not just the dreams upsetting Joseph; it was something else, "getting even," Maggie said. "You still want to get even with him."

Maggie had talked it all out with Tom Spencer who had in turn talked it over with his wife, who had reported a conversation she had with Joseph; one in which Joseph had "volunteered the information" (Maggie's phrasing) that he would retaliate for his cat's death by finding the killer's most vulnerable point and then attacking him there.

"Let's hash this thing out!" Maggie had insisted the night before last, "You've got it in for Janice's husband and you won't admit it. I thought it would stop with that little dinner party you fixed up, but no, no! You've got it in for him!"

"Foolishness," Joseph had answered.

"Oh yes? Throwing out the fly-swatter is foolishness too! Trying to find out the number of doctors who murdered since 1900 is foolishness too! That man didn't kill a person, you know, Joseph; he killed a cat! You're making a mountain out of a molehill. Personally, I think you're plain old-fashioned cracking up!"

"You're the one losing control," Joseph had answered. He had wondered how many people right at that moment in the world were falling apart inside; everything in them crumbling, yet the body's façade contriving to keep the same calm, not even a slight flicker of fear in the eyes, nor a trembling by the mouth, but everything intact. Were they hearing the truth screamed at them too, piling another avalanche on top of the quivering debris of busted emotions inside, while somehow they stood there making the mechanical rebuttal sound real? "You're the one losing control"—saying something like that to their accuser, their definer? And why was it, Joseph wondered, that he could not simply say, "Maggie, yes, I'm losing control." Would it have brought a cool hand to the head, comfort?

Dear is the tear, the wind soft-voiced, the peaceful word. Is there peace in you?

"No kidding!" Maggie had ketchuped the hash. "You're sick, Joseph!"
"Sure," Joseph had answered with a wry smile of disdain, a pot-calling-the-kettle-black expression; and he had remembered in that moment some fragment from a poem, read when?

> *. . . sleepwalking on that silver wall,*
> *the furious sick shapes*
> *and pregnant fancies of your world . . .*

Now he was here in the driveway of the Hart house, at the fork in that road with the pointers: "Office," left; "Home," right. He went left.
"Ask him right out if he killed your cat, and tell him it made you angry!" Maggie had said the other night.
There was good sense in that suggestion; good sense shined in Maggie's world like the sun. Joseph could remember the time Maggie's Uncle Avery died. Avery had been the only person Joseph had met through Maggie whom he had really cared about. They had been together seldom, on Avery's rare trips to New York, but Joseph had felt a warmth for this wise old man, which he had experienced so rarely with anyone, that he came to regard Avery as special. As was always true with Joseph, he never conveyed the feeling to Avery or Maggie, yet he sensed Avery knew he was appreciated; he felt almost as though Avery were a much older brother, a father even. Maggie had always smothered her uncle with expressions of affection; Joseph not. Yet when they had set off for the funeral in Schenectady, it was Maggie talking a mile a minute all the way, and Joseph wondering if what he felt tight in his throat was not a horrible gasp wanting escape, a stifled noise of bereavement, not a sob, but a wail, the way some old Jews moaned their grief, a sound of pain and not self-pity. The funeral parlour had smelled of

flowers, the sweet sickly odour of them was like a command to the dead to have the gumption to sit up, hold your nose, or stay forever insensitive to insensitivity; and Joseph had felt a rising panic, anticipating Avery's features frozen with that dread finality. He had followed behind Maggie and even before he had seen the body, he had heard the sound of her weeping, seen her run across fearlessly, bend over Avery, take his meaningless flesh in her hands, pucker up her lips and press them on his. This ritual done, she had turned to Joseph, to beckon him closer, and Joseph had stood there, rooted to the spot on the rug where he had paused on entering the stinking room, a smile, unbidden and uncontrolled, spreading over his countenance. It was as though the smile were some brazen intruder, manipulating Joseph's mouth, misshaping his face. Joseph had stood there that way, with Maggie staring at him. Maggie never stopped saying, "You laughed when Uncle Avery died. I saw it with my own eyes! You didn't even have the common sense to pretend you felt bad!"

Joseph parked his car beside a pick-up truck. Next to the truck was the black Mercedes. For a moment, Joseph stayed behind the wheel of the Ford, tapping the Physical Examination Certificate on his knee, the tan form which was his excuse for being here. The Commonwealth of Pennsylvania required a doctor's signature on Joseph's application for a licence. In addition Joseph had brought with him a book, gift-wrapped by the shop in New Hope from which he had ordered it a week ago. It was a psychological study called *The Unknown Murderer*, by Reik.

On the flyleaf, Joseph had written:

"For your contemplation, from Ishmael, a Siamese who used to live on Old Ferry Road."

It was certainly not Maggie's way of doing things, but for Joseph Meaker, it was the closest thing to saying it right out.

Chapter Eight

Disorder.

The word flashed through Joseph Meaker's mind the second he stepped inside the doctor's office; one quick look around licked the label, stamped it across the room.

"Joe, Joe, glad you dropped in."

"I should have phoned."

"No, the hell with formalities. What can I do for you?"

"I brought my driver's certificate."

"Aha! Sure, we can do that for you, Joe."

Louis sat down at his small roll-top desk in the corner, his back to Joseph, fussing through papers, humming to himself. Disorder everywhere. A stethoscope flung on a chair, needles nesting in a towel on the window sill, an empty bottle of iodine overturned on a cabinet top, a pair of rubbers scattered about on the floor with an umbrella, and near the door a stack of old magazines.

Joseph was neat. Maggie said he had "a thing" about being neat. Cats were neat too. Dogs would step in their own dirt and keep right on going, oblivious to it, but a cat who had such an accident shook its leg irritably, walked, stopped, shook it again—nine times out of ten, cleaned herself. Joseph had always respected cats for their neatness. He had always been careful about Ishmael's pan, not to let it stay dirty, and Ishmael knew and appreciated. The moment Joseph would dump the pan, and rattle the bag with the fresh litter, that cat would come running from wherever she was.

"I was wondering when I'd see you again, Joe."

"It's been a busy time." The trick was to act matter-of-fact; let Louis Hart look back on this moment and remember how cool Joseph had been. Joseph told of his visit to the cloisters in Ephrata, last Monday. A man named Beissel had founded a religious order there in a quest for solitude, for flagellation of the spirit. What Joseph saw as Cocalico Creek, where the settlement began, was once the snake-infested Kock-Halekung, a barren and dangerous spot where Beissel took up his life of self-attrition. Joseph had been deeply moved by his visit there, but he kept emotion from his voice, and recited the details of his visit in a mundane fashion. In his Journal at home, he had written: "Beissel's loneliness is my own. I too will escape one day, so far into myself that I will be free of self; isn't that what Beissel meant?"

"Ah, yes, Ephrata!" said Hart, nodding his head with a nostalgic air, as though he were every bit as involved in the cloisters as Joseph. Joseph hated him for that. He wanted to sneer at Hart, ask Hart what *he* knew about it.

Instead he simply said, "I saw some interesting petit point in Lancaster County too. Much of it harking back to the French Huguenots' influence." Joseph had in mind a particular embroidery, with the distelfink woven in, and the roses and lilies surrounding the red and goldish ecru legend from Psalms: *"By this I know that thou favourest me because mine enemy doth not triumph over me."*

"I've always thought Beissel had the answer," Louis said.

"I imagined *you'd* think he was crazy," Joseph said with a small smile of contempt. If Louis noticed it, he seemed unaffected.

He said, "Let's hear the old ticker, Joe. Undo your shirt."

Joseph was glad Hart had called him Joe. It was a name as unfamiliar to Joseph as some stranger's, and he was glad Hart could not achieve an intimacy even in the little way of using his first name.

Joseph's heart began to pound as he undid his shirt. Sometimes when he was reading late at night in his study, with the house quiet, he would hear his heart in this same way. It made him feel as though his own self were standing over him, regarding him, deciding about him; his own self who knew him best, better than Joseph knew himself. For a second while Louis pressed the ear of the stethoscope into Joseph's flesh, Joseph had the thought that now his self and Louis Hart were working together, listening not to his heartbeat, but to those inner thoughts even Joseph never heard. It was a nervous second's sensation which made Joseph flinch momentarily, prompting Hart to say, "Steady;" then Joseph heard his heart race faster, thumping and protesting. It was his self rebelling at the intimacy with such a man; *that* was it.

"Racing a bit. You nervous, Joe?"

"I've been working very hard." The lie came easily. It was a wonder to Joseph. He had never been able to lie, not even in a matter of no consequence; yet there it was, spoken without a tremor. Since he had visited the Ephrata cloisters, he had not translated one note into so much as a paragraph. Usually he was quick to record his impressions, but the room he worked in was too great a reminder of Ishmael, and though he had tried to set up his work on the kitchen table, his reason for being displaced that way carried him off into a fit of brooding.

Maggie never realized what was happening to him, not really. His preliminary paper on the "German Sectarians of Provincial Pennsylvania" had gone so rapidly that Maggie had suggested he keep it a few weeks before submitting it. Maggie had an idea people did not respect the fast worker; sometimes Maggie dragged out an idea for weeks, wrote up dozens of little memos before the coup. Joseph had ignored the suggestion, but when he won the grant for this new study, Maggie said her strategy had paid off. "Take it easy with this new project, too," Maggie had said, "All the early bird ever *does* is get the worm!" For Maggie there was no end, no means: the strategy justified the strategy. If Joseph was not working lately, Maggie undoubtedly imagined it was strategy.

Louis was winding up the stethoscope into a ball, pushing it aside on his desk. He was murmuring to himself as he looked over the card. "Let's see, not a narcotic addict, not an uncontrolled diabetic, not an uncontrolled epileptic, not an—"

Not a killer either, Joseph felt like saying.

"I can skip the urinalysis, hah? This is just so much red tape." Louis scribbled his signature at the bottom. "If you drank, I'd offer you a whisky. I'm about finished today."

"I haven't anything to let loose," said Joseph.

"Hmm?"

"People who drink usually have something to let loose. I don't have."

"Oh? Well, okay then, Joe." Hart handed him the form. "That's it."

"Thank you." Joseph had left the gift of the book on the chair by the door, in a plain paper bag. He got up to get it, stumbling into the pile of magazines.

"My past," Louis said. "I'm a miser. I hoard the past. These are *Life*'s from 1948." Louis leaned over and picked up one of the magazines, slapped it across his desk top. "I sit here and go over them." He sighed. "Nineteen forty-eight's my favourite year. Lots of progress. Chicago hotels got Gideon Bibles with alcohol-proof covers in 1948."

"I remember that year very well," said Joseph.

"People were singing 'Nature Boy' and reading Dr. Kinsey. Gandhi was assassinated, and the Department of Commerce instigated National Laugh Week."

"I was still in college," Joseph Meaker said.

"*. . . and my dear, I love your soul—profound, sad, wise and exalted, like a symphony.*"

"What do you remember?" said Louis.

2

He remembered 3 May, 1948, standing on the Boone County Courthouse lawn. The sun is hot, but it is not a hot day. Spring in Missouri.

Signs:

> WALLACE'48
> HENRY WALLACE FOR PRESIDENT
> WALLACE-TAYLOR

Beside him a farmer is holding a coke bottle, empty, holding it back by his shoulder. Coca-Cola. Joseph stares at the word. Coca hyphen Cola. He has never noticed the hyphen before. He knows what the farmer is going to do. He could reach out with his own hand and wrestle with the farmer for the bottle, prevent him from throwing it, but he is loath to involve himself. There would be a fight. There will be one anyway; that's right, and he is wearing clean clothes. He wants to leave. In the stacks of the library this very moment there are other students studying in the neat cubicles, row on row of them, like monks; sheltered, protected by the shelves of books. His own books are there in the cubicle reserved for him, five, six, seven, neatly arranged on top the metal desk; and in the drawer, sharp pencils, fresh paper, waiting there as

66

faithfully as any cat or dog waiting for the master. He
wishes he were there with them. He stares at the white
hyphen wishing this. Coca hyphen. Then the hyphen sails
up, disappears; there is a fist in its place now, and around
Joseph, more fists, like spears on all sides. Now chanting:

BLACK NIGGERS ARE RED NIGGERS!
RED NIGGERS ARE DEAD NIGGERS!

Singing follows:
> *We don't want him,*
> *You can have him,*
> *He's too red for us!*
> *He's too red for us!*
>
> *We don't want her!*
> *You can have her!*
> *She's too black for us!*
> *She's too black for us.*

On the platform Henry Wallace tries to shout above the
noise; behind him the Negro woman speaker stands
straighter, holds her head higher, her glasses glinting in the
sunlight.

Joseph recognizes the tune. At the boardinghouse where
he lives an Indian student sings at "she doo fat for me, she
doo fat for me." Beside Joseph the farmer cries, "Go
back to Russia."

Students to the left of Joseph chorus, "What about
Russia?"

Henry Wallace tries to answer, "I admit I could not get
free speech in Russia. I say to you who are denying it to
me here—"

A chorus of boos, jeers. Joseph is pushed backward
suddenly by the crowd's boisterous movement. Someone
has stepped on his shoe, a heel of dust insults the high
shine. ("Don't be afraid to get involved, Joseph, because
you are already involved; all mankind is involved in the
people's struggle. You must just face it"—lying in bed
beside her last night, she had said that.)

A vendor selling lemonade is knocked against a tree.
The lemonade spills on his white uniform. Joseph can feel

its stickiness just as though it were his own clothes soiled. Joseph knows how it smells right now in the library, the green odour of the liquid used for mopping the floors, balanced with the musty smell of the L-M books near his cubicle, and the faint aroma of Vicks Vapo-Rub which Clarence Somerville in the cubicle behind Joseph puts in his nose for his year-round cold. ("I hate violence! In the war I was a C.O., Varda! Because I hate violence!" The bedsprings creaked; she leaned over to get a cigarette, lighted it; the smoke spiralled up between them in the darkness. "Put your hatred to use in a good way, or it will choke you, Joseph. One day it will get out of its big bottle, and you won't be able to control it then.")

Suddenly a tall girl with hair yellow like Varda's and eyes deep blue and fierce, rips at the neck of the man in front of her. "Rubble!" she screams. "Scum! This is a democracy!" Blood trickles at his hairline, down to the dirty collar, while surprise and shock stuns him only for an instant, before he grabs her blouse with his large hand, tears at it while she digs her nails into his face. Students pull her back, and others hold him by his arms. "Rubble! Scum!" she yells, and her blouse is open in front, her breasts thinly covered by the nylon bra. The man being held laughs, a leer cuts across his face, and in a sudden lurching that takes all his strength, he wrenches free, pulls the bra, catching her in a quick jerk that brings a wide-eyed cry from her. He steps back, laughing. The girl covers herself. An angry young man comes forward swinging his fists, and is met by opposition.

"She started it!"

"Let me kill him!"

"Kill you, college boy!"

"Dirty—bastard! I could—"

Joseph looks for a break in the crowd. On the platform the Negro woman is speaking. A tomato hits the podium. Jeers. Chants. Men with dirt-encrusted wrinkles, eyes narrowed from squinting; boys with peach-fuzz new beards carrying books, girls in skirts and sweaters oohing, ahhing, milling together restlessly; and on the courthouse roof a grinning skinny boy holding up a hammer and sickle. Joseph finds space to move, starts his way back through the crowd. ("Don't leave me yet, Joseph," she had said last night.) Someone with a cigarette bumps against him, knocking the cigarette's ash on Joseph's light-blue wool V-neck sweater. He smells the burn, rubs it out with his thumb. A woman hisses at the Negro speaker, the spray of her anger falls on Joseph's cheek; he rubs that out too, as though it were a leech fastening itself to him. When he can run, he does. He does not look back for Varda. He knows she is standing in the back with the other workers, passing the collection box among the rabble.

Later in his cubicle he hears Clarence Somerville behind him, blowing his nose. There is peace in the sound; music nearly. A contentment envelopes him; dust of old books in L-M dance in the dying rays of late afternoon sun. Joseph thinks a poem in his head:

Let my own music to the clouded mountains lure me,
Past festered sores that stare in mortal grin . . .

He scribbles his poem on a piece of scrap paper, knowing he will never finish it; it is all he cares to say. It is not so much that he was afraid back there at that rally; it is that he could not see himself in anyone there. That was it! *That* was it! He feels better now and works until the library closes.

"So you just walked out on it," she says that night. She is carrying her shoes. She has sneaked up the stairs of the boardinghouse for their date. "I know it was awful for you."

He does not want to talk it out with her. He reaches for her and brings her to his lap on the bed, kisses her face. Kisses away crumpled papers on the courthouse lawn, crushed paper cups, the crowd exercising its ugly democratic right: kisses away older memories, her brother murdered in Pest by Nazis, barbed wire world of her youth; Jew-girl taunts; forget it, Varda, now let me touch you; he feels a tenderness breaking his heart open, spilling a gentle desire all through him for her—then she holds him back.

"You went to the library, I suppose."

"Yes."

"You're so weak, Joseph."

"I hated it there."

"That word again. Hate."

"Didn't you hate it there? What they did to that Negro woman! And I saw a girl whose blouse was ripped by—"

"Never mind."

He watches her undress. She has golden hair and she keeps her eyes open, and once she told him to watch her eyes, that he would see himself in them.

"Anyway, it was a very successful rally. Very!"

"Successful?" He lights her cigarette for her. Sometimes she does this, sits on the bed smoking a cigarette, while he undresses.

"Very!"

"But they were all booing, singing those disgusting take-offs on songs. She's too black for me! Successful?" He doesn't like to sit naked. He keeps his undershorts on.

"We wrote those take-offs, Joseph. We started everyone singing them."

He laughs. It's a joke.

"I mean it! Dick Gilman from St. Louis got the idea. Mob psychology did the rest. We just started the ball going, as you say in America."

"Why?" Still he grins at her; it's crazy.

"To get people sympathetic to Wallace, the Negro woman. You wait. The newspapers will be full of it tomorrow. Free speech was denied. A Negro woman was humiliated. It was disgraceful, happening at a big university! I saw Professor Hutchens in the crowd. He looked as though he was going to be ill, he was so upset. Don't think he won't have something to say to all the students in his classes tomorrow! Don't you see, Joseph? Wallace and the Negro woman were martyrs! We'll get some votes just because a few people who witnessed this are ashamed!"

"It makes me sick!" Joseph says finally. Suddenly she is more naked than he has ever seen her; than he ever wanted to see her. A conniver on his bed, legs crossed, smoking. The end justifies the means.

"Maybe *I* don't want to sleep with *you* tonight," he says.

"If you mean that—"

"No." Still it is different now. He looks at her.

"You're disappointed in me, Joseph. I wish you

weren't. I wish I could explain it to you so you could understand. I'm so happy with you. So depressed every time I have to leave you. Yet we *are* worlds apart, in so many ways." She stubs out the cigarette and takes his hand.

"The cause is more important than that Negro woman's feelings?"

"Yes. We did it *for* her."

"I don't want to talk about it any more."

"Put it in the big bottle again then. But remember, Joseph, there won't be any more room in there one day. You'll stuff it until it bursts."

"Don't talk tonight," he says. "Please."

3

"What do I remember about 1948?" Joseph answered. "It's of no importance. What does it matter?" He reached down and picked up the paper bag, with the book inside. He remembered how Ishmael always liked to crawl into empty paper bags, roll them over and over from inside. When the newspapers began printing stories about children suffocating inside plastic bags, Joseph had made Maggie promise never to bring one in the house. He was afraid she would forget, get careless one day and bring cleaning home in one, so he reminded her often. Once it angered her into snarling that he had an obsession about something happening to that cat. "You ought to find out the reason for it," she had told him, not in a nice way, either. It was as though she were keeping something from him, something she knew about him that he did not know about himself. Women were often mean that way.

Louis Hart said, "You have to forgive me, Joe. I live in the past."

"I do, too," Joseph said. "The near past." He held out the paper bag. "This is for you."

"What is it, Joe?"

"No, don't open it now. When I go, open it."

He saw the look of puzzlement on Louis Hart's face. He remembered the last shuddering of the cat's broken and bloody body; the blue eyes asking why before the blank stare of death impaled them; and he did not feel

71

sorry for this man. He could not say anything more to him except good-bye. Yet as he walked out of the doctor's office after saying that, he felt the moment was very much like a book he had read once, where the author had begun with the words "The End", and finished with "The Beginning".

Chapter Nine

He took the long way home because he had to think. Maggie was arriving from New York that night with Amos Fenton, one of A.& F.'s account executives. Although it was not yet five o'clock, Maggie often left after lunch on Fridays, and she had said something that morning about wanting Amos to see the countryside on the way up. He did not want to chance finding them at the house before he had thought everything out. He had felt tense and strange at Louis Hart's office, but that sensation was being replaced gradually by a feeling of light-heartedness nearly euphoric now. Wasn't that because he had finally managed to get the whole thing off his chest? Maggie liked to talk about getting something off your chest. It was Maggie's theory that Joseph's chest was hopelessly weighed down, "like a camel carrying Rockefeller Centre around," she sometimes put it. "Get it off your chest, Joseph." That expression always reminded Joseph of the legendary incubus, the nightmare who rode his victims in the dark, or sat straddling them until they were breathless from the weight. But by now Louis Hart had opened Joseph's gift; he knew, by now. He was probably sitting in his messy office going back over the whole course of events in his mind, from the moment he had first seen Ishmael in his headlights, to the moment Joseph had approached him in the Doylestown Shopping Centre, to the present: this afternoon, near dusk, on the second of December.

Joseph was approaching the beginning of Tidd's Woods. He was not far from home now, and he was not yet ready to face the noise and Amos Fenton and the nervous aura of New York Maggie always brought with her.

Joseph turned on to Old Ferry Road, having gone two miles in a circle from Louis', approaching his home the other way now, still not ready to arrive there. He pulled over to the side of Tidd's Woods, cut the motor, and sat looking out at the huge red eye of sun sinking off in the west between the trees. He should simply forgive Louis Hart, as soon as Hart called and apologized. Wasn't that all Joseph really wanted, to hear the apology, to believe it was sincere? Joseph had always been disturbed by the stories in folklore of revenge. The avenger was often more cruel than the offender by his way of retaliation.

Would Hart call that evening? "God, Joe, I'm sorry about your cat. I never realized—" Say something like that?

Joseph might say, "I'm not going to forget it, Hart. Don't think I am!"

Let him stew then; let him wonder what Joseph meant, worry about how Joseph might repay him in kind. Was that enough? Joseph might say, "Thanks for calling, Hart. Now all that's left is for me to think of a way to even up the score."

A green station wagon pulled up in front of Joseph's car. The man who got out was carrying a gun; pinned to his back was the Celluloid shield containing the regulation hunting licence. He nodded at Joseph as though Joseph were a colleague of some kind, then he trekked off into the forest. Joseph could see the bright colours of a dead pheasant piled on boxes in the rear of the station wagon. When the man was out of sight, Joseph opened his door and got out. He wanted to see the poor dead bird, to despise the hunter all the more by witnessing the bullets' ravishment of the animal's body; but when he looked in the station wagon's window, he saw no blood on the bird, nor any wound, merely its lifelessness and its eyes squeezed shut in its last pain.

Joseph stared at the magnificent colours of the bird, the intricate blending of them, the fabulous beauty there. He remembered the ugly pock marks on the hunter's face and his big, clumsy and pot-bellied body. He thought of the hunter's death some far-off day when loving hands would prepare him for display in some satin-lined coffin, lay out his last crisp white handkerchief for the pocket of his suit, select a proper tie, and shine the shoes for his feet, lay him softly down and surround him with lilies and low lights of flickering candles, and weep for him. How much more beautiful this bird would look in the hunter's casket; how much more fitting that the hunter's bulk be thrown atop a pile of boxes in the back of a station wagon.

Joseph opened the station wagon's back door and took

out the pheasant. He carried it gently to his own car, and placed it with a certain tenderness beside him on the front seat. When he reached the house, he would bury the bird, put him to rest quietly in the ground, beside Ishmael. He would forgive Louis too when Louis called to apologize. There was too much violence; too many people all out of control everywhere. A slight shiver went through Joseph as he started his car. He was thinking of where his own anger could have led him, if he had not right at that moment near Tidd's Woods, decided to forgive Louis Hart. He felt control come back to him. It was all right now. He felt nearly gay and certainly calm. Only when he passed the spot where the Benz had struck down Ishmael did he hear the faint thundering of his own heartbeat. But what could you expect?

2

"Imagine this," said Amos Fenton. "You are going through a room filled with people you respect. Now I mean, you really *care* what these people think of you! Okay? And you happen to overhear them saying something about you. Got it? All right. What I want to know is, what most would you like to hear said about you?"

Maggie said, "Amos, what a wonderful question! God, give me time to think."

Naturally, Joseph Meaker said nothing. Good God, but Maggie had picked herself a lemon! Fenton poured himself and Maggie another brandy. Meaker was sipping ginger ale in an orange-juice glass. Behind Maggie the fire danced over the logs in the fireplace; there were long white candles flickering on the table between Fenton and Maggie, and Amos Fenton had a sudden sorry wish that Joseph Meaker would simply disappear from his place at the head of the table.

"You think, too, Joseph," said Maggie.

"I don't have to," Joseph Meaker answered. Fenton thought of how he would like to pick up Meaker's glass of ginger ale, and spill it over Meaker's head. Maggie deserved better, for damn sure!

Still, he kept his composure and said to Joseph, "In our

75

business we *have* to wonder about people's self-images. But this is a good question anyway, for anyone to answer! It shows you a hell of a lot about someone."

Maggie said, "Do the people in the room know I heard what they said?"

"No, Mag, that's the point. It's not the point, but what you *hear* is an absolute frank statement about you. Now what would you like to hear? It can be anything! You pick it."

"Amos, I love it! It's a great question!"

Amos Fenton beamed. He looked straight into Maggie's eyes, way in, hoping she would know by that look how goddam much he really thought about her. Fenton was a widower of two years, a man in his late forties with two boys, the oldest fourteen. He had transferred from Barton Beam Agency to A. & F. a year ago, and on sight, he had liked Maggie. This was the first time he had ever been in her home. On the drive up, Maggie had said, "You know my husband might scare you a bit at first. He's sort of solemn and introverted, but you'll get used to him." Joseph Meaker did not scare Amos Fenton; he made him want to puke. As far as getting used to him—Fenton would sooner warm up to one of the kooks from A. & F.'s mailroom.

"I think I know the answer," said Maggie. "What I'd like to hear said about me is that I had heart! It's as simple as that, Amos!"

"Honey, that's easy for *you*. And it's a hell of a good answer!" Amos Fenton held her glance some fraction of a minute, smiling at her—God love her—wishing he could reach across and put his large hand over her hand.

"And how'd you answer it, Amos?"

"Me? Well, Mag. I'd like to hear something like this. 'There goes Amos Fenton. That's a fellow with real character!'" Fenton sat back and laughed, "Hell, I mean, why not? I'd like to hear that." He acted embarrassed, but he was actually quite pleased. He felt a warmth with Maggie; he felt as though Maggie thought he *had* character, the same way he knew Maggie had heart. Joseph Meaker could go jump, for all he figured in that moment, just go jump.

Instead, Joseph Meaker said, "You forgot the salad again, Maggie."

"Oh, who the hell cares?" Maggie took a sip of her brandy. "I always forget the salad."

"Why do you make it and let it go to waste?" said Joseph Meaker. He took the salad bowl from the table behind him, spooned some on to his plate. "It'll just go to waste. Doesn't anyone else want any?"

"We're having brandy, Joseph."

"All right. All right."

Amos Fenton said, "Hell, put it in the refrigerator. I like day-old salad even better. Have it for breakfast with my eggs." Meaker's face was sullen, and Fenton could feel Maggie fidgeting across the table. To relieve the moment, Fenton said, "C'mon, Joseph, you haven't answered the question. What would you like to hear?"

"I don't care what people say," Meaker said.

"Well, there you have it!" Maggie said. "Old Mr. Personality himself!"

Amos could not control a sudden guffaw, but he turned to Meaker afterward and said, "Oh, come on now, Joseph. Surely there's something you'd like to hear."

"Why is there?"

"Well, everybody wants some kind of approval, for the love of Mary!"

"Don't be hateful, Joseph," Maggie said. Maggie looked good in that sweater. Fenton did not care if she saw him look at her there with pleasure. He could no more imagine Maggie in bed with Joseph Meaker than he could imagine Garbo with Wally Cox.

"Hateful?" said Joseph Meaker. "Where do you get the idea I'm full of hate?"

"Why don't you answer the question then?"

"I don't drink."

"What's that got to do with it?"

"Yeah," Fenton said, "what's that got to do with it?"

"People who drink always end up saying personal things. Just because I don't drink, I don't have this compulsion to unburden myself!"

"Well, *aren't we nice!*" Maggie snapped. "Mr. Snug and Smug!"

Again, Fenton guffawed, harder this time. He saw Joseph Meaker flinch as though the noise hurt his ears, but Maggie was laughing too now, so he did not care. Maggie began to sing a song to the tune of the Mr. Clean commercial:

> *Mr. Snug hangs on to all his thoughts,*
> *He never tells a soul them,*
> *He takes a little shovel out*
> *And buries in the hole them!*

Both Maggie and Fenton chorused: "Mr. Snug, Mr. Snug, Mr. Snug!"

Joseph Meaker got up and walked into the kitchen area. He turned on the small light over the sink. Then he took the ginger ale bottle and carefully poured back into it the amount left in his glass.

"Come on, Meaker," said Amos Fenton, "we're only pulling your leg."

"Come on, Joseph, come back and join the party."

"It's late anyway," said Meaker. "I have some notes to go over."

"Joseph, it's not even eleven o'clock!" Maggie said, but Fenton kept his mouth shut. Why encourage the creep to stay?

"It's the noise!" Meaker whined.

"Oh, the *noise*, Joseph! There're only three of us, and we've hardly spoken above a whisper!"

"You're mistaken, Maggie. I doubt that we could even hear the phone ringing; it's been *that* loud!"

"Who's going to call us?"

"Someone might. It's only an example," Meaker sighed.

Maggie snickered. She said to Fenton, "Amos, are *you* expecting a phone call? Because I don't know who in the hell would call *us* up!"

Amos Fenton sensed the despair of embarrassment in the wisecrack. He was glad that Joseph wished them both good night at that point, and disappeared up the stairs.

3

At eleven o'clock, Lou was "in". He and Janice had once seen a Tennessee Williams play where one of the heroes described Lou's feeling as "hearing the click in your head," but for Lou this full transition from sobriety to intoxication was an ingress to a shelter, not easily accessible either. Once "in", nothing could make a dent; "in" had no memory.

This particular shelter was housed in the Danboro Bar, and he had found it after four Scotches there, and countless Scotches back at the house. He had poured his first Scotch after opening the "gift" from Joseph Meaker. He had looked at the cover, tossed the book in the wastebasket, and poured number one. He was somewhere around five or six when Janice came back to see why he wouldn't answer his phone. She had stood there giving him hell, and he had listened to the whole harangue with a certain boredom, until Stilt peed all over his pile of magazines. Everything snapped then. He went for the dog in a rage, kicking him a couple of times, with the dog squealing and Janice screaming; then Janice and the dog left him alone, and all the way up the outside walk he heard Janice telling the dog in babytalk about locking out the old nasty.

The Danboro Bar was as warm and crummy as Lou had remembered it from years ago, when he stopped in often on his way from Doylestown to Point Pleasant. Some of it was like old times. Even Alfred White was still bartending, and there were still no stools to sit on at the bar, and the jukebox was five years behind the times, as always. A few men were shooting pool in the back room, and the framed faded print of Bruegel's "The Return of the Hunters" was in its same place, over the cash register. The ways it was different now, Lou Hart knew, had nothing really to do with the bar, but with what people thought. Every time Lou ordered another, for instance, Alfred simply shrugged and said tartly, "Okay, you're the boss." Some of the men waved and hi'd him; others said nothing more than what the sour expressions on their faces said.

But Lou Hart was "in"; he didn't care.

There was one fellow though, Duncan something, from

over in Lambertville—Lou and he got to talking. He had come across to hunt, took his vacation every year in the fall, near the end of the small game season. He was an ugly, pock-marked, tubby fellow, but Lou was glad for the company, and they had lapsed into long free and easy talk about women, automobiles, house-buying, sports and marriage. He was a mayonnaise salesman, ex-Marine, and around eleven they were still talking away, about the year 1944 by then, both several sheets in to the wind, and Lou saying, "Sure, and there was a movie called 'A Guy Named Joe' that year. Spencer Tracy and Van Johnson."

"Yeah, I remember seeing that on ship."

"And 'See Here, Private Hargrove,' that year," Lou said, "A great year! My favourite! I remember this song—how'd it go? Ummm—let's see, 'I thought I'd call you up this morning because—' " he hummed the rest of the tune and Duncan snapped his fingers and said, "I got it! 'I Couldn't Sleep a Wink Last Night.' Dinah Shore!"

"Right," Lou laughed. "That's the one—then there was 'Poinciana,' and there was one called—"

Duncan interrupted him suddenly, "If you live on Old Ferry, you live near Tidd's Woods, huh?"

"That's down at the other end."

"I was hunting down there. I got a pheasant over in Carversville, then I come to Tidd's Woods for some squirrel. Parked right by the side, and when I come back to my car, damn pheasant's gone."

"How come?"

"Search me—I think some guy took it. I mean, there was a guy there when I pulled up. I think he must have swiped it. Some bastard or something, I don't know!"

"The next time," Lou said, "listen, the next time, you park at my place, 'kay? You leave your car my place. Dr. Louis Hart. It's right at the other end. We have a lot of migrant workers getting the old corn out this time of year. It's not safe to leave your car around."

"Thanks."

"Just leave it behind my house, see? There's a parking spot, you'll see it."

"Thanks, Doc. I want to get some deer Monday."

"Sure. You do that."

"I don't think it was a migrant worker. This fellow I

pulled up in front of wasn't no migrant worker."

"Well, they come up from the South in a bus. Work three, four days this place, three four, the next."

After that they discussed Tommy Dorsey, and the year Chuck Klein hit four homers in Shibe Park in a major-league game, and near eleven-thirty they were laughing about the old double-O advertisements for Listerine Tooth Paste, back in '41. Offensive breath; offensive-looking teeth: too bad for Davey, he had the double-O!

The argument began over something silly. Who blew up the U.S. battleship *Maine* in Havana, 1898? When Duncan banged his fist down on the bar and declared flatly that the United States of America would most certainly *not* blow up a ship full of its own boys, just to get into a war, Lou Hart said, "Don't be stupid!" He was bored by that time; he was thinking of taking off. He saw Duncan's eyes then; Duncan looked out of his head.

"What did you call me?" Duncan wanted to know.

"I said, don't be stupid."

One thing led to another then, and in minutes Duncan was telling Lou it was Lou who was stupid; any doctor of medicine who would stand around in some dumpy tavern getting himself soused was stupid, Duncan said, and Duncan said Lou was *some* doctor of medicine, he *just bet*, when Lou grabbed him by the collar of his jacket. Lou's fist connected with Duncan's nose, and was on its way back to score a second time when Alfred White had him by the arms from behind.

"Now, get out, Doc! Just clear out!"

Duncan was standing there nursing his nose with a hurt expression in his eyes.

"Stay out of here. Is that plain?" Alfred White asked Lou.

"Yes, it's plain," Lou said. He walked across and got his coat, everyone in the place watching him now, with a silence like a fog, smothering the atmosphere. He banged the door shut behind him, and crossed to his car. Parked beside the Benz was a green station wagon: Lou took the flask from the glove compartment of his car, and had a long swallow. When he was corking the flask, he saw Duncan come out of the bar and walk across to him.

Lou's window was down, and Duncan poked his head in.

"Shake, Doc?"

Lou shook. He turned his key, began his motor.

Duncan said, "That's what my wife always calls me, 'stupid!' She had herself a year in some lousy junior college and she thinks she's Einstein. It's a sore point."

"Sorry," said Lou.

"Yeah, we both flew off the handle, Doc. Let's forget it. Friends?"

"Sure," Lou said.

"I appreciate your offer to let me leave my car at your place, too."

"Sure thing," said Lou Hart. He pulled out and started down towards Gardenville. He glanced at his watch, ten-to-twelve, and he put his foot on the gas pedal. There was a place at the crossroads near Gardenville that stayed open until twelve.

4

. . . is dead and dumb and done.
Never more to peep again, creep again, leap again,
Eat or drink or sleep again—
Oh, what fun!

Amos Fenton burst into laughter when Maggie finished reading it.

"But it is sweet of Joseph, isn't it?" Maggie said, "Come on, Amos, you have to admit that it is sweet of Joseph!"

The door between the upstairs and the downstairs was not shut.

Joseph sat in his armchair in his study letting their raucous conversation rape his peace. A letter from the Varda file lay on his lap, a piece of yellowing tissue paper now, but a moment ago words warm and real, plunging him back in time, caressing him:

"You know well, Joseph, that I love the symbolic language, and your little poem would get directly where it meant to get, to my heart—and awake feelings seldom felt before and dreams and understanding and vows. Above all, a little insight into your dear soul, to which I in my

blind selfishness, am so often unjust. It is good to imagine that your sweet face, beloved to me, must be in this same moment inclined on that piece of paper—"

"Sweet!" Amos Fenton roared, "Hell, he ought to have his head examined! Aw, Maggie, I'm sorry I didn't mean—"

"I know you didn't."

How did she know he didn't? Joseph wondered. Was it so easy for her to know him? He didn't even have to finish sentences. He just had to say "I didn't mean—" and Maggie would say, "I know you didn't." The Flents for Joseph's ears were across the room on his bookcase. If he got up to get them, would they hear him? Call him downstairs? Or would they let him walk about alone all he wanted to upstairs, as though he were not even there? Which way? Both were awful to imagine, so he stayed in the chair.

Amos Fenton was saying, ". . . think that he's a nice enough guy, but not for you. Maggie, I just don't get it!"

"He's brilliant, Amos. The Pennsylvania Society of Folk Mores has—"

Amos did not wait for her to finish. "Brilliant doesn't warm up the home on cold nights, does it, Mag? Oh, hell, I'm sorry. I didn't mean—"

Joseph waited and it came, predictable as the next beat of his heart.

"I know you didn't," Maggie said.

"This brandy's got my tongue, I guess," said Amos Fenton. "Mind you, I don't disagree with what it's making it say, but I don't seem to be able to control it."

Joseph heard the sound of a light slap then, followed by Amos Fenton's voice, very confidential in tone now. "Maggie, just tell me something. Are you happy?"

Joseph imagined Fenton's hairy hand resting somewhere on Maggie. It was not exactly jealousy but a twinge of some other sort: injustice? Another affront for the Josephs of the world? Right now were there thousands of Amos Fentons placing their hands on the Joseph wives, with the Josephs mute, and the Amos Fentons counting on the fact that the Josephs were always mute?

"Happy?" Maggie said. "I wonder if I know what happiness is."

"*. . . and this is what they mean by happiness, Joseph, to feel the blood circulating gayly and self-consciously in my veins, and you the life to my pulse. . . .*"

Amos Fenton said, "Well it's belonging. It's when you belong to someone and something. Hell, I think it was Shakespeare who said we're just a pair of halves apart, but together we're scissors. You know?"

No, Joseph said to himself, it was Dickens. It was from *Martin Chuzzlewit.* "We are two halves of a pair of scissors when apart, Pecksnifi, but together we are something."

"Together we're scissors," Maggie said, as solemnly as she might have said "The Lord is my shepherd."

"Aw, Maggie, Maggie, I wish so much for you."

Did he have his arm around her now?

"You're sweet, Amos. You're very sweet."

There was a moment's pause. The next thing Joseph heard was the sound of Maggie's heels as she crossed the living room. Then: "Joseph is probably sleeping by now," she said. "Let's shut the door so we won't disturb him."

Chapter Ten

He was at that stage, in the zenith of intoxication, when one decides: I *am not at all drunk.*

From Gardenville he had called Janice and she had said sarcastically: "Oh, you sound fine! Really in great shape! How do you manage to hold your liquor so well, Lou?" He had hung up on her, deeply insulted, and he had driven along the Plumstead Road thinking that his so-called drinking problem was all in Janice's head. He drank. He admitted he drank. He laughed, delighted with everything suddenly. He felt so absolutely clear-headed. Moreover, he felt a certain closeness to his Benz; indeed, a camaraderie. He had read once in a psychology journal that paranoids often shut out the world by creating an imaginary one of inanimate objects: an old maid might name her fountain pen or her teapot, an eccentric gentleman might name his bathrobe or his footstool. With a certain whimsy he thought that perhaps he ought not to postpone the naming of his Benz any longer; why not join the ranks, after all; but the thought was striped with a distant sadness, one that did not touch him at the moment, but one that could if he were to give in to it. It had something to do with spoiling his life, with the mess his life was and everyone in it, with the fact the Benz was the only perfect thing he had—perfect, beautiful, functional. Respectable.

"Respectable," he said aloud.

Then he became somewhat taken with the graceful manoeuvring of the car; with the car's grace, and with his own deft handling of the car. More proof. He was absolutely, incredibly, fantastically sober. When he made the turn onto Old Ferry Road, he looked for lights in the Meaker house, fully expecting to find the place dark. It was after one now. The last thing in the world Lou Hart wanted to do was go home. Go home and have Janice's baby-talking with Stilt assaulting his ears. It would be much worse tonight, he knew. It was always worse when he was drunk. He corrected himself. When Janice *thought* he was drunk. That was her punishment for him, now that

Tony was gone and they weren't there to confront him together. *Stilt-zun, booboly-boo, tum away fwrom baddy ole smell of liquor, booby!*

But there *were* lights on in the Meaker house. Downstairs, at that.

If he were drunk, of course, it would be a bad time to settle the matter; but sober, what was wrong with it?

Nothing.

He turned in at their drive.

He got out near the back porch, but the lights were on in the front, in the living room. He decided to try the front doorbell, and he walked along the side lawn, pausing by the first window of the living room. The last thing he expected to see, he saw. There they were necking on their couch. Well, it was a night of mystery, it was, and all the better that they were in a good mood! The other thing that caught his eye was the brandy bottle on the table. He would take it easy with them, be sure they offered him a drink first.

He pressed the doorbell twice, feeling guilty about the second ring. He knew he wanted the drink more than he wanted to settle anything with them. The drink was important because here was the night half shot and here he was dead sober. Right? Right! Then the porch light went on, and he could see Maggie with her hands cupped around her eyes, peering out of the narrow windows beside the front door. He gave a wave, and called, "It's me! Lou Hart!"

He shuffled his feet and clapped his hands together against the cold, and it seemed some minutes before the door opened.

"Lou?" Maggie said, looking straight at him, still asking, "Lou?"

He went past her and inside, although she had neither stepped back to let him pass, nor invited him in.

"Hi, Maggie!" he said. "I was just passing and I saw your lights."

He went directly into the living room, holding his hand out to shake with Joe (the drink, *first*, remember) and instead of Joe, he saw a grey-haired fellow in his shirt sleeves, with a crooked Countess Mara bow tie under an

86

Adam's apple the size of a tulip bulb. The fellow looked annoyed, particularly as he smiled broadly and said his name. Amos. Lou had wanted to name Tony that, after a favourite professor; but Janice had looked the name up in some baby-naming book and discovered it was Hebrew for "a burden".

"Is anything wrong?" Maggie said.

The Burden was lighting a cigar, standing up, as though he would sit down *after* Lou left.

"Where's Joe?" said Lou.

"Joseph's in bed," Maggie answered. "Oh, *you* know *Joseph!*"

"No, no, I don't."

"Well, I mean, Joseph never stays up late. Early to bed, early to rise—that's Joseph."

"Am I intruding on something very private?"

That worked. Maggie said, "Oh heavens, no, Lou. Have a drink, if you'd like one. Amos and I work together in the city." She made no move to get an extra glass from the kitchen. She said, "We were just talking over an account."

The Burden said nothing, and still stood. Lou unbuttoned his coat. "I'd like the drink," he said. "Thanks, Maggie."

Maggie left him with the Burden for a moment and the Burden asked him what field of medicine he specialized in, and Lou decided to say he was a proctologist. Well, wasn't he?

"I'm afraid you lose me there," the Burden said.

Lou wanted to say "Promise?" but he was sober, by God, so he kept up his half. "Diseases of the rectum," he said.

The Burden's face was properly repulsed. "How does a man come to choose *that* field in particular?"

"Why not?" Lou said. "He gets *piles* of satisfaction from it!"

Maggie was back with a brandy snifter and a nervous smile then; and Lou was disappointed when she poured in a small amount of brandy, and handed it to him saying, "Here's your nightcap."

Then it went along all right for a while with how's Janice, she's fine, isn't it cold, not as bad as some years, and a discussion of Hurricane Diane in 1955, winds up to

75 m.p.h., the River Road to New Hope flooded under, and Lou's brandy was gone. Lou reached for the bottle since no one was offering a refill, and the Burden said,

"Maggie's very tired, Doctor. I think we'd better give her a break and call it a night."

"Right after this drink," said Lou.

"Look, *Doctor* Hart, I can't make it much plainer. Maggie's tired." He held his hand on the brandy bottle, just below Lou's hand.

Maggie said, "I'll bet Janice is worried about you, Lou."

"One for the road," Lou said, and with a jerk of his arm, he had the brandy bottle out of the Burden's grasp. He uncapped and poured, while the Burden said, "It's pretty unfair to Maggie, Doctor. I'd make it fast, if I were you."

"Are you always fair to Maggie?" Lou asked him.

"I *try!*"

"How about to Joseph?" Lou said.

Maggie was on her feet now, rushing over to sit beside Lou. "Now, you've probably had quite a night for yourself, Lou. Don't you worry. Just take your time and then we'll bundle you off to Jan. I know she's worried about you."

"Did she call up or something?"

"Well, no, but—"

"Then how do you know she's worried about me? Do I look like a sheep dog?"

The Burden was clearing his throat for some special pronouncement. Then he stood up again. "Doctor, I'll help you with your coat."

"Sure, well, you just stand there holding it, and when I'm ready, I'll snap my fingers at you."

"Oh, Lou, I hate to see you like this," from Maggie.

The Burden was right behind him now. Maggie was telling him please not to be hard on him, and the Burden was saying well, we have to get rid of him right now, don't we, or he'll pass out here.

"If he's going to pass out," said Maggie, "I'd rather he stayed the night on the couch. He could have an accident."

"Don't worry about *their* kind, Mag. They get home every time!"

Lou was looking up from one to the other as though he were a spectator at a tennis game, watching the ball dancing between the pair, and he was quiet because it occurred to him that while they argued, he might pour himself another. The Burden had the same thought, apparently, because the next thing he did was pick up the brandy bottle and take it into the kitchen.

Maggie said, "Lou, do you want me to call Janice?"

"What for?"

"I'm worried about your getting home."

"Do you think I'm drunk? I came here absolutely sober. I came here to settle something with Joseph."

"What did you want to settle, Lou?"

He knew that the Burden was purposely lingering in the kitchen, out of sight but within earshot. If Lou could convince Maggie he was all right, she might make the Burden bring back the bottle.

So Lou plunged. "I want to know what connection Joe has with the Tondleys."

"Who?"

"The Tondley's. They're a farm family near Mechanicsville."

"I've never heard of them, Lou."

"And Joe?"

"He doesn't know anyone who lives out this way. We both came out here without knowing a soul."

"Who suggested the move?"

"Lou, really—"

"Did Joseph?"

"I think he did. He got this grant from the Pennsylvania—"

"Never mind that! That's what *he* says! Did he know Freddy Tondley?"

"Lou, Lou, you're really talking about something I don't know one damn thing about! I can't—"

The Burden's voice interrupted her. He was standing in the entranceway, between the kitchen and the living room. "I think we've had just about enough, Doctor Hart!"

"Freddy Tondley was in the Marines!" Lou shouted at

Maggie. "Was Joseph ever in the Marines?"

Maggie Meaker began to laugh.

2

"Joseph in the Marines! *Jo-seph!*" . . . Well, let her laugh. And didn't Amos Fenton sound authoritative though, with his "*we've* had just about enough." . . . Joseph stood behind the door to the downstairs, on the bottom step, listening.

Some time after Maggie had closed the door between the upstairs and the downstairs, he had fallen asleep. He had been sitting up in his chair and a violent drowsiness had overtaken him. Then there was another dream of Ishmael, another dream re-enactment of some random moment in the cat's life; this one, the time Ishmael had suffered with the ingrown toenail. Joseph had taken him in the carrier to Dr. MacKellar. That was all, simple and meaningless. Yet when Joseph had awakened from the dream, he had felt tears come to his eyes. He had gone into the bathroom to wash his face, and it was then, on his way back, passing the upstairs landing, that he had heard the third voice—Louis'.

Joseph had crept down in his stockinged feet. They were all talking about the water-line on the River Road, after Hurricane Diane. Joseph could not figure out how Louis had ever suddenly appeared there, until later on in the conversation he caught the thickness in Louis' speech. Louis was there drunk, to apologize at last, was that it? He had thought so; he had nearly come out from his hiding place when Louis had made the remark about settling something with him; but then Louis had changed the subject abruptly. What did the Tondleys have to do with Joseph?

On an impulse, Joseph gave the door a slight push.

Then he said, "Maggie's very tired, Doctor. You heard Amos say so yourself. She shouldn't laugh so hard."

Fenton came across to him and said out of the side of his mouth, "Look, Meaker, how about helping me give this guy the heave-ho? He's stinking!"

Joseph stepped down and into the living room, facing Louis.

"Why should I know Tondley?"

"You know his name! I thought so!"

"I was listening. That's how I know his name."

Maggie said, "Joseph, have you been eavesdropping?"

"Freddy Tondley!" Louis was shouting, "Conqueror of Iwo Jima, hero of Taejon, caught in an electric saw in Mechanicsville, P.A. How about it, Joe? He a pal of yours? Was he?"

"I never had a pal, Louis. Not even a dog named Pal. My cat's name was Ishmael. That means 'wanderer.' One night he wandered into the headlights of a car. Right here on Old Ferry Road, Louis."

He saw Louis' eyes, the same glary look there he had seen the night Louis had come to dinner; glary and somehow dead-looking too, fixed to nothing, but moving in their sockets as though they could see what was in front of them. It disgusted Joseph; at the same time it made him slightly fearful. They were like the eyes of someone gone soft in the head.

Maggie sounded angry. "Just say it right out, Joseph, damn you! Don't beat about the bush!"

And Joseph saw that Maggie's eyes were that way too; she had been drinking brandy all evening down here with Fenton. Joseph looked more closely at Amos Fenton. His eyes were like agates, cold and hard. Joseph realized it was fury he saw written in Amos' eyes.

Was everyone out of control? Joseph felt a shiver run from his back to his neck. Louis was crossing the room, coming toward him slowly.

Maggie said, "Never mind, shut up, Joseph, don't say anything!"

"Have you got anything more to say to me today, Joseph? Or did that little book say everything?" Louis was standing so close to Joseph that Joseph could feel his breath on his cheeks.

Joseph said, "It's you who should say something to me, isn't it?"

"Was Freddy Tondley your friend?"

"I don't even know him."

"Do you think I murdered him?"

Joseph had no chance to answer. At the same time Louis asked that question, Maggie said something to

Amos Fenton; the next thing Joseph saw was Fenton's hairy arms grabbing Louis from behind.

"I want you out of here," Fenton said. "Now!"

A small smile tipped Louis' lips. He said to Joseph, "Do you want me to kill your wife's lover too? Is that it, Joe?"

Then Fenton socked Louis, and Louis socked Fenton back, and Maggie began screaming, "Not in here! Not in the house!"

Joseph turned and started across to the staircase. His last look was at Amos Fenton, red in the face, a repugnant leer snarling his features into a confusion of ugliness, while he grunted in the effort of punching Louis Hart's nose.

Joseph thought to himself, there goes Amos Fenton. That's a fellow with real character—and he went upstairs, the house coming down with the noise.

Chapter Eleven

On Saturday morning, Amos Fenton had a black eye, and a sudden recollection of something he had to attend to in New York, immediately. He was full of saccharine apologies about having to cut short his week-end and Maggie received them with all the seriousness of a civilian in war-time, confronted with a soldier's recall to active duty. Joseph watched the scene impassively, for as long as he could stand to; then he went up to his study and read a dissertation on *gruttafoos* until Fenton's car pulled out of the drive.

When he was sure that Maggie was occupied with the breakfast dishes, Joseph sneaked downstairs and went out by the barn to bury the pheasant. He had told no one about having the poor dead animal; would there be any point in it? The new December ground was hard, but Joseph punctured it with the pitchfork, finally, and made the bird's grave beside Ishmael's. He was glad the bird's remains would rest intact under the dirt, glad he had saved the bird from having its feathers picked, its head and legs chopped off, its insides pulled out, and what remained cooked up for the prongs of its killer's fork. Joseph resisted the temptation to save one of the beautiful feathers; it belonged with the whole beauty of the animal; it was a part of the animal.

Joseph would have liked to paint the bird before he had buried it. He thought of going into the house for his drawing pad and sketching it before he covered it over with dirt; but the thought seemed as cruel as the thought of eating the pheasant. It was dead; let its loveliness be lost to the world now; let the world receive no gratification from *this* slaughtering.

"Where were you?" Maggie said when Joseph returned to the house.

She was making a pot of fresh coffee, using Risestaver's, one of A. & F.'s accounts for which she had written the copy. For coffee that cries flavour, use Risestaver!

"Out walking around," said Joseph.

"Walking around with a pitchfork?"

"What did you ask for, if you saw me?"

Maggie said, "For all I know you were digging up the cat to send parcel post to poor Lou Hart."

Joseph got a cup down from the sideboard. He hated the coffee. ("What do I crave for? Risestaver!") He liked Martinson's in the blue can, but Maggie always said Martinson's was not putting any money in *her* pocket, so why should she put any in theirs!

"Well, what *were* you doing out there with a pitchfork?" said Maggie.

"Burying a corpse," Joseph said.

"Oh, ha, ha, and ha, ha! Aren't we funny this morning!"

"I guess it's a carry-over from last night," said Joseph.

"I was wondering when you'd start on *that!*"

"On what?" Joseph saw the coffee start to boil; began timing it, since Maggie never let it boil a full twenty minutes, as he liked. ("Want a lifesaver? Have some Risestaver!")

"For one thing," said Maggie, "I think it is perfectly awful that you had to give Lou Hart a book like that, instead of coming right out and telling him you knew he killed Ishmael!"

"He didn't even apologize."

"He was drunk! He was not in his right mind, Joseph! I told you last night, that Lou Hart was out of his head last night! Why else would he say that absolute nonsense about Amos and me?"

"I can't imagine." ("I'll be your slave for Risestaver!")

"Well, think for yourself, *please*. What was all that about the Tondleys? Who the hell are the Tondleys, or this Freddy Tondley? He didn't know what he was talking about!"

"Maybe he murdered someone by that name."

"I'm getting very tired of all this talk about killing and burying a corpse and murder. I am! I mean, if I hadn't been analyzed, I wouldn't mind all this talk, but I just happen to know that it's one big cover-up for hostility! And I don't like it one single bit, Joseph!"

"Tell Louis, not me."

"You're goading him into talking that way! Now, Joseph, you have to face the goddam fact that Lou Hart killed a cat! Not a person! A cat!"

"I'm facing that fact."

"Oh? Are you? I suppose you'd rather he'd killed a person? A friend?"

"He wouldn't have the courage to kill anyone who could fight back."

"Just drop it, Joseph! Just drop it! I don't want to talk about it."

"All right."

"We just won't talk about it."

"Fine."

"That's *your* way. Just keep it all inside of you. Isn't that your way, Joseph?"

"Yes, I think that's my way."

"Think? *Think?* You're probably standing there right now brooding about what Lou Hart said with regard to Amos and me! Instead of talking it over with me, you're probably standing there right now making a mountain out of a molehill!"

"I wasn't giving it any thought at all," Joseph said. This morning, before he had read the dissertation on *gruttafoos*, he had looked into the Varda file for the photograph she had sent from Venezuela. For a few minutes he had studied it, the face of each one, with the names printed underneath: Varda, George, Aniko, Katricka. He had taken his thumb and put it across the faces of George, Aniko and Katricka, and there was Varda alone, looking back at him. ("Am I dear to you? Dear is the shadow, reflection of us—") On Varda's shoulder there was the hand of George, which he could not cover with his thumb, without covering her.

"You pretend you don't care, Joseph, that's *your* trouble! If you could only admit that you care! You can't even admit it to yourself!"

"I thought we were going to drop it?"

"You'd like to, wouldn't you? Never face up to anything, Joseph—that way you'll always be safe! Don't drink, because you might give yourself away! Don't smoke, it might relax you, and you daren't let down your

95

guard! And whatever you do, don't live in the present, because it's so much less demanding back in the past with Varnish!"

"I don't know what Varda has to do with anything."

"I don't either, but don't think I don't know you sit around up there reading over her old letters! She's a communist besides!"

"*Was*," said Joseph.

"You're always carrying on as though you were Mahatma Gandhi, with your non-violence and conscientious objectoring, and who was your big heart-throb? Some communist!"

"The coffee's done," said Joseph ("Won't you stay for Risestaver?")

"Someone who believes in bloody revolutions!"

"I said the coffee is done, Maggie."

"And I said she's a communist! And Joseph," Maggie said, waving a spoon at him like a finger pointing naughty, "don't think you would have fallen for her if she hadn't been one! You can't admit your aggressions *or* your hostilities to yourself! That's why you get someone who admits hers all over the place. Like me! Then you can sit around and pet the cat, and good old Maggie will let off enough steam for both of us!"

"The phone's ringing," said Joseph.

Maggie held the spoon under his nose, wagging it like a hopped up metronome. "Oh, you could use some analysis, Joseph! If it wouldn't do anything else for you, it might give you the gumption to answer the phone in your own home, instead of telling me about it!"

2

Saturday noon he was sober. He woke up at The Washington Crossing Motel, outside Trenton, New Jersey. Across the room the television was playing. He must have pulled in here late last night, but it could just as easily have been early this morning. The Late Show sometimes lasted until two or three in the morning.

His last recollection was of the bar at Danboro, of going in there and ordering a drink, of Alfred White wiping glasses by the cash register, under the framed print of Bruegel's "The Return of the Hunters." After that? Nothing.

His best guess was that he had called Janice. There had been a quarrel. He had decided not to go home. That was the usual pattern. Then he would drive across to New Jersey, where he was not known, pick some out-of-the-way motel, register under another name and sleep it off.

There was a bruise on his jaw, and one on his nose. They were not painful and he had not noticed them until he had looked in the bathroom mirror. A fight or a fall? He examined his clothes but found no clue, nothing torn or soiled. Lou Hart was bored with analysing the reasons for these bouts; he had stopped doing that long ago. Guilt, in any recognizable form, was also not a part of these experiences, nor was self-reproach. He no longer strained to remember the details of the blackout period; it was a waste of time. When this happened to him, he just got on with it. It seemed neither pleasurable nor painful—though some of the past bruises had been physically painful—but oddly enough, this happening gave him something nothing else could: a purpose. For as long as it lasted, his energy was concentrated on a single objective: drinking. There was no alternative; by now he knew that, consequently, no indecision nor any back-and-forth reasoning. Like any other state of emergency, the commitment was only to the exigency.

In the shower he thought about Meaker coming to his office and leaving the book. He had dumped it in the wastebasket without a second's thought, save for the horrific impact of the title's implication. He sensed Meaker's meaning without thinking about it; he poured his first drink before he wondered how Meaker figured in the matter. His second drink did not tell him, nor his third. That was the start of things then—that had triggered this bout. Lou Hart knew that even before Meaker had arrived, he had been spoiling for this anyway. It had been a long time, and perhaps too long. Whatever it was anyone wanted to call it—escape? some sort of self-punishment? plain old alcoholism?—it had not ended last night; it had begun. Lou Hart knew that. When he had shaved and dressed, he would drive to a package store and get a couple of fifths; stop at a delicatessen and buy some food.

Then call his answering service, cancel the rest of the day's appointments, have them call Janice. The doctor is detained in New Jersey. Janice knew how to translate that message; more than likely, so did the answering service by now.

Outside it was a grey damp day, not too cold for December. He noticed with some sense of satisfaction that his car was parked at a proper angle in front of his cabin, and that the windows were rolled up and the door locked. His keys were in his right pocket of his overcoat, thirty dollars in cash in the left. Another relief; he would not have to write a cheque; he would not have to worry that the name he signed on the books might not tally with his credentials. His licence plate said he was a doctor. Doctor who, was anyone's guess.

At the office, he explained that he was staying over. He paid for another night in advance, and was on his way out the door when the woman at the desk said, "Do you want the maid to clean up your cabin right away, Dr. Tondley?"

His shock at hearing her call him "Tondley" left him dumb and blank-faced. He stood staring at her.

"I said, do you want the maid to make up your room right away? She usually does it at three, but if you're coming back before—"

"Yes," he said, "right away." Then he said, "Did you say Tondley or Tonley?" He walked back to the desk. He wanted a look at the card he had filled out last night. She held it in her hands and he could not make out the writing.

"Tondley. T-O-N-D-L-E-Y."

"Let me see?" he said.

She handed him the card. His writing was large and uneven, the way it always was when he was "in." He had signed Duncan Tondley. Above it, on the top of the card, she had typewritten the name.

"You see," said Lou Hart, "it's really Tonley. I made a mistake. I was just curious."

"I'll change it, Doctor."

"No, it doesn't matter all that much. I just wanted to see the card."

She gave him a wry little smile. She had thick glasses, so thick that Lou could see only whirls and spools of glass where her eyes were. "My husband said you was awful tired or *somethin'* when you checked in," she said.

He thanked her and went out to his car. He knew, of course, how the name Tondley had come out, but the Duncan was an enigma. He knew no one by that name. It was a silly name, one he never thought about.

3

Joseph often thought back on that night with Varda, after the Wallace rally, but even *that* did not help him Saturday evening. Maggie sat up and lit a cigarette, and switched on the radio beside the bed. A giddy chorus of women were singing about the fact that a customer at a certain bargain centre had "all next year" to pay for Christmas presents. Joseph reached for a pamphlet he had been reading earlier that evening, a study of the Persian origin of the pomegranate and other "Dutch" motives in painted tinware.

"Well, I just hope he's home by now," Maggie said.

The phone call from Janice Hart, at noon, had snapped Maggie's mood from one of nagging anger to one of maudlin sweetness. The news that Lou Hart had not come home all night had launched Maggie on a sea of sugar-coated clichés.

"I guess we never know how fortunate we are until we hear how unfortunate others are," was one of them.

Another: "We may not have the perfect marriage, but we're a lot better off than some people, aren't we, Joseph?"

She was very nearly elated. It repelled Joseph. It reminded him of times past when she would have this same reaction after a horrible plane crash, or an earthquake, or a close friend's divorce. She would change from the strong Maggie to the weak Maggie, affecting a certain togetherness with Joseph which had an undertone of desperateness, as though they were shipwrecked together, and stunned somehow into a perverse sense of gratitude at the fact that they had a three-day water supply.

"What are you reading, Joseph?" she said.

He began to read aloud, "Like so many motives in our art, the pomegranate harks back to an East more easterly

99

than Biblical lands, to Persia, where—"

"All right! All right!"

He knew he was not behaving in any way that went along with her present fantasy about them. "Well, dear," he should have said, "this is a very fascinating pamphlet on 'Dutch' motives. I think it would interest you to know that—"

"Sometimes," she said, "he goes off for days without a word to Janice. She told me that. I'd leave him flat, if I were Janice!"

"I feel no sympathy for her. What did she let him kick the dog for? If they want to fight between themselves, let them, but why does an innocent animal have to be involved!"

"I knew if I repeated *that* part of the conversation, that's all you'd remember. Here a man—a doc-tor, has gone off drunk and no one knows where he is, and his wife is frantic, and you think of the goddam dog!"

Joseph turned the page of the pamphlet as though he were reading it. All day he had been turning pages that he had not read, just going through the motions of life. He had a headache too; he had not had a headache in years, not since those days when he would drink alone; wake up the next morning to find a strange packet of matches on his bureau, or the blood on his collar; unable to remember where he had gone the night before. He could very easily have turned into a Lou Hart, had he not brought himself under control. Those days were unreal to him now; he could not imagine himself that way. He believed he very possibly might have been suffering from a nervous breakdown of some kind, without even knowing it. Only his sharp instinct for self-preservation had saved him. He thought of it now as a "stage" he had gone through. When his headache began at noon, he was shocked by it, for it was a surviving trace of a time past. Something else shocked Joseph Meaker, a dream he had had last night. It was funny that when he had awakened he did not remember it; but at noon, when he picked up the butter knife to spread jam on his toast, it came back to him.

He had dreamed of Dr. Saperstein, his dentist, the man who had stood up for him when he married Maggie. Saperstein knocked on the front door in the dream, and when Joseph opened it, Saperstein said he wanted back the gold stickpin he had made for Joseph.

"That's not very fair," Joseph had told him. "It was a gift."

"But you never wear it, and I need the gold for a filling."

"I will wear it!" Joseph had protested.

Saperstein had smiled in that polite way of his and answered quietly, "No, you won't ever wear it. You're afraid to. You're afraid people will know you carry a knife."

It was one of those illogical dreams, the sort Maggie was always repeating at breakfast, and Joseph almost never experienced. It bothered him, like some nasty buzzing fly in the bedroom at night. For a while it would go away and he would forget it; then it would dip down into his consciousness again and annoy his concentration.

Beside Joseph in the bed that night, Maggie was still carrying on a conversation. With herself, for all Joseph's part in it.

". . . and then I remember the time there was that big jet crash over in Staten Island, and what did *you* say? You said, 'I bet there were animals on that plane.' That's what *you* said. That there were probably animals locked in the baggage compartment! Never mind the people being burned to a crisp! Let's all cry over Fido!"

"There are always animals on planes," said Joseph. "I see nothing strange in the remark."

"You see nothing strange in anything about yourself! Strange people don't!"

"That's their compensation for being strange perhaps," Joseph said.

"Animals on the plane! That's you, in a nutshell!"

". . . *and my dear, I love your soul—profound, sad, wise and exalted like a symphony.*"

Joseph felt a sudden fatigue, accompanied by the familiar loneliness. The only intruder was the headache. He got up and walked down the hall to the bathroom. Because it was Saturday night, near midnight, he very nearly expected to hear Maggie's voice coming from the downstairs, when he passed the landing. He realized that he wished he could hear it, that he wished he could walk back into the bedroom and find no one there but Ishmael. Let Maggie have her great downstairs, and he would have his upstairs—and in the crook of his arm his cat would curl up, and it would be the way it used to be. Going down the dark hall, Joseph Meaker wished he could cry, cry as he had that night when he had picked up his pet from the road, and held it to him in its last breath of life. Now there was just this tender fullness inside of him, this huge aching that struggled for motion, this formless sensation waiting at the threshold of his control, like the genie not yet come to life in Aladdin's lamp.

Chapter Twelve

On Monday morning Joseph woke up with the same headache, to the noise of Maggie on the telephone. It was ten minutes to seven and Maggie was telling someone that something was one hell of a goddamned good idea. Was it Tom Spencer calling? Amos Fenton? Was it about Risestaver Coffee? Picks Cigarettes? And was this to be the third consecutive day of the headache? Joseph lay on his back staring up at the ceiling, thinking about everything. All day yesterday Maggie had tried to get him to say he was not jealous of Amos Fenton. Joseph had refused, knowing that once he said he wasn't, Maggie would imagine he was.

"Lord, Joseph, we're old buddies, Amos and I."

"I think that's fine," said Joseph.

"Then why the long face? Then Saturday night?"

"My face has always been long; it's a characteristic of my face. As for Saturday night—those things happen."

"Don't you even wonder *why* they happen?"

"Not unless I think it's about to be a matter of permanency."

"Well, *I* can tell you why. You think something went on between Amos and me while you were upstairs Friday night."

"I see."

"So what if we have a few drinks and act a little affectionate! We're very affectionate people. Amos and I are a lot alike. Some people are cold as January, and some aren't; it's just not their natures. They're warm and outgoing!"

"Good for them."

"Yes, *good for them*! It's no reason to sit around and look daggers at someone all weekend."

"Was I?"

"*Were* you?"

Joseph turned over in bed, trying to shut out the memories of yesterday's conversations with Maggie. It was not that they annoyed him per se; quite the contrary. They seemed to have nothing to do with him, yet he knew somehow he was involved. Towards the end of Saturday and then all yesterday, Joseph had felt an estrangement from anything and anyone around him. He had the headache, for one thing; but it was more than that. It was a feeling of simply not caring, not being interested—not in Maggie or his life with her—not in Lou Hart or what was happening to him—not in his work—not even in his daydreams or the Varda file. He had moods in the past which bore a thin resemblance to yesterday's, but there was a difference. In the past, it was emptiness he always felt, a hollowness. Yesterday he had felt full, nearly brimming over with something. Whatever it was, there was an urgency about it that would not let him sit still and read, or work, or paint, or do anything in any way distracting. Joseph likened it to the days back in college when it was almost time for Varda to come to his room, but not quite. During that small space of time he waited, he was never able to do anything. He would listen for her, imagine what it would be like when she got there, then listen for her, then imagine, then listen, and on and on until she was there. Yesterday was like that, wasn't it? It was as though he were waiting for someone. Never mind who, what, why—that was Maggie's kind of asinine analyzing; it was just the feeling he had, the fact that *that* was what it was like.

As he lay in bed wondering if his headache would persist that day, he thought of going somewhere; perhaps that would help. He had a second's thought that he did not want any help, that he wanted only to let something come about (but what?) and that he must wait and be patient and it would. The thing was, he could not bear the headache and that seemed to be part of it. He decided to go to the cloisters in Ephrata, to have another look at them. In his mind he pictured the blank, grim and grey buildings, their steep-pitched roofs and worn, patched sides, as bare of paint today as they were two centuries ago. He remembered the doorways of the cloisters, five feet high only, built low to teach humility; a foot and a half in width, in reminder of the straight and narrow way. Inwardly he snickered remembering Louis Hart's comment that that way of life was "the answer." Hypocrite—with his Mercedes Benz and his three-day drunks! Oh, the hypocrisy! He hoped Louis Hart would run his Benz off the road! Yesterday Janice had phoned to say he still was not home. Joseph was unable to care. It was simply another annoyance, the same as Maggie's periodic announcements of her non-involvement with Amos Fenton. And today? How did he feel today?

Maggie appeared in the bedroom then, a cigarette dangling from her lips, her face fresh with the excitement of whatever it was that was one hell of a goddamned good idea.

"Well!" she said, "that was Janice!"

No matter the news, Maggie was the type of person who revelled in being its bearer. Joseph remembered one night when he was working in his study, and Maggie had rushed up from the downstairs to announce Clark Gable's death to him. The fact that she had been the one to bring the news gave her a certain air of personal involvement with the movie actor, and she sat beside Joseph rattling off Gable's triumphs and telling of how an era had passed, offering to get Joseph a cup of hot coffee; then coming back with the coffee for more talk of Gable. She had colour in her cheeks and a flash to her eyes, and Joseph could see she was in the midst of a heady excitement. He remembered wondering what that was like, that feeling; and whether it was good or bad? Somehow it depressed him, he remembered.

That morning after Maggie announced that it was Janice on the telephone, she sat beside Joseph again, on the bed this time. It was like a monologue, "Well, why shouldn't she?" she said. "He finally phoned again and said he was coming home. Well, Janice isn't going to be there, that's all! She's going to ride into the city with me. We'll need the car, Joseph. And she's going to have a nice day in the city! Shop and have lunch and the hell with him! What should she do? Wait quietly with folded hands until he shows up? Then make him breakfast, I suppose. Well, that's what *he* thinks! I don't blame her one single—"

Joseph sighed and realized he could not go to Ephrata. The cigarette between Maggie's fingers was burning down dangerously close to her flesh, and it startled Joseph. He waited, watching it, and when it did burn her, she brushed her skin absent-mindedly and ground out the cigarette in the ashtray. She was that out of control! He had seen her do that when she was drinking, but now it was simply a case of sheer excitement that insensitized her. It gave him a strange feeling, in the light of all that was happening around him, a feeling that everyone was letting go, in little ways and big ways, and only he was still hanging on. To what? His headache was very bad now. To myself, he thought; I'm hanging on to myself. Maggie was telling him she was going to fix French toast for breakfast, as a special treat. She was pulling her nightgown over her head, telling him they would have thick bacon, the new pure maple syrup she had ordered from Vermont, and French toast! A special treat, she repeated. In honour of the fact Louis Hart is coming home to find his wife gone, Joseph thought; in honour of the fact Maggie is so wildly happy at others' misery that she cannot feel her cigarette burn her. He tried to remember something from the Varda file, something to take his thought off this moment, but he could remember nothing to appease himself. He felt a strange nervousness start to invade his thoughts, so that they were all mixed up. There was one thought that stood impervious to the confusion, the thought that everything was a façade. In his mind he pictured a castle's façade; he had seen a hamburger house on the road from Trenton, with a castle's façade hiding it from view. A huge many-towered golden castle, and behind it, a squat little hamburger stand. Was that the sort of façade he meant? A big one with nothing behind it? Or was it one of an entirely different nature—one that looked innocent and was treacherous. Lou Hart's face. Maggie's—Amos Fenton's—his thoughts began to race, mixed-up, crazy. His headache, worse. Across from him Maggie was naked before the mirror.

"God," she said, "I'm getting stretch marks."

2

After Maggie left, Joseph was alone for two hours. Again he tried to read without success. He made some notes on the pamphlet about the Persian origin of the pomegranate, which he had looked at Saturday night, but he realized that he had read it without concentration and he could remember very little. He remembered that for Christmas Maggie had said she would love a sketch of the house, and he thought of taking his sketch pad out and starting to work on it, but her attitude that morning had so disgusted him, he could not bring himself to do that for her. For a while he sat in the living room wondering if everyone was like Maggie, or if Maggie's ways were unique. Callous. That was the word for her. For everyone as well? It seemed so; look at them—begin with Tom Spencer and his grovelling after money, accounts, a place on Madison Avenue; remember him sitting up all night to gripe about his wife not understanding him, callous at her loneliness upstairs, waiting for him to come to bed. Louis Hart with his immaculate Mercedes Benz, his filthy hole of an office; killer-doctor, that was a doctor, for you, wasn't it? Ah, Amos Fenton—there goes Amos Fenton, a fellow with real character. Take Janice Hart, take—God! Joseph got up and walked across the living room. Music. That was what he needed. Music.

He chose Bach. *Christ Lag in Todesbanden.* He thought of nothing else but the music. He listened to the brooding, solemn start of the *Sinfonia*, then sang a bit with the chorus. "*Er ist wieder erstanden*;" his hands conducting the melody, oblivious, oblivious—until the third verse, until those words "*da bleibet nichts den Tod gestalt*", with the violin's brutal four-part chords. He could not stand to listen any longer. Was everything taken up with violence, brutality? Everything? Death? Strip death of its power—ha! Ha! He began to laugh, but he did not want to; he felt himself doing it, but he deplored it. Then as soon as it had started, he stopped it. He would put his hat and coat on and take a walk. He felt reassured by his decision not to stay in the house. It was all right to be nervous, and he was not blaming himself, but he was not going to let it get out of hand.

He was outside about twenty minutes when he saw the man walking towards him. There was something familiar about him, he could not think what it was. As the man came closer, Joseph saw that he was carrying some rope in his hand, that he was wearing a heavy outside flannel shirt, high boots that laced, and a battered brown fedora.

He waved at Joseph. By the barn, Joseph waited for him. Then when the man was nearly within six feet of Joseph, Joseph remembered where he had seen him. At Tidd's Woods last Friday. He was the man whose pheasant Joseph had taken. A shiver went through Joseph. The man was standing right in front of him now—but he was holding out his hand to shake with Joseph, and he was smiling. A trick?

"Hello? Name's Billy Duncan, from over in Lambertville. Wonder if you'd do me a favour?"

"What is it?" said Joseph.

"I been hunting down in Tidd's since eight-thirty. Got a deer back there. I put my gun across it, but I had some trouble that same place last Friday, and I don't want to leave my gun or my deer too long." The man smiled again. "So I was wondering if I could drag my deer here? Leave it while I get my car down the way?"

He was ugly. Joseph thought of the pheasant's feathers while he looked at the pock-marked face, the tiny yellow-brown teeth the man had, like a row of old corn. Joseph looked down at the rope in the man's hands, and the man followed his glance; then said, "I damn near got myself killed getting that deer of mine bound. Thing was kicking still when I come up to it. Some boys get killed that way."

Joseph said, "A deer." He said it without thinking; he was thinking how loathsome the man was, calling himself Billy like a child, talking about "my deer" and "boys," like *himself*, Joseph supposed; this man thought of himself as little Billy Duncan out getting a deer all his own, brave little Billy Duncan who found his own little deer kicking just a bit from all the buckshot, before he died.

"Yeah, a nice one. First day's always good."

"First day?"

"Deer season. Guess you're not a hunter, huh? I seen your land was posted. Well, I myself sometimes don't like taking some of them. Little rabbits. Kinda hate to, myself." The man was tossing his rope from one hand to the other. "And I don't blame you for not wanting people trooping all over here with guns."

"If you don't like to kill little rabbits," said Joseph, "why do you?"

"Hfh? Well, I—I'm a hunter, Mister."

"You live that way?"

"Well, now, no, but I'm a hunter, just like any hunter! I mean, a hunter don't go thinking he ought not to kill rabbits because rabbits is any different from other animals. They ain't."

Joseph noticed the way the man slipped into sloppy speech; ain't now, instead of aren't. He knew the man did not say "ain't" often, only when he was little Billy Duncan, trying to be cute about being a big hunter.

The man said, "Hell, now, I don't want to get into any argument. You don't want me bringing my deer here for just a few minutes while I get my car, then say so, Mister."

Joseph said, "No, bring your deer here." He was looking at his shovel and pitchfork beside the barn. He was thinking he would bury the deer, the same way he had buried the pheasant—the same way he had buried Ishmael. When the man came back, he would tell him he saw some boys in the yard, but he had not watched them closely. The boys might have taken it, he would say.

The man was thanking him, telling him he would leave it out by the drive, adding it was a job to haul, but he could do it alone he guessed. Then he walked away, back in the direction he had come. Billy, Joseph thought. Billy! He spat; it was like a bad taste in his mouth, the man's name.

When the man was out of sight, Joseph went around and started breaking ground with the pitchfork. He chose the back of the barn to do it. No one could observe him, and there the deer would rest beside Ishmael and the pheasant. The ground was hard; it would take him a while. He would probably have to hide the deer inside the barn, then bury it when the man was gone for good. Joseph put all his strength into the ground-breaking. He realized when he got up his first shovelful of dirt, that his headache was gone. In its place was a sensation almost as odd as pain, a sensation of euphoria, wild pulsating euphoria. He began to sing the Bach he had been playing earlier: *"der Würger kann uns nicht mehr schaden! Hallelujah!"*

At the man's voice, he looked up, startled.

"What're you digging, a trench?" the man laughed.

"What are you doing here?" said Joseph.

"I knocked on your door and when there wasn't any answer, I heard you singing, so I come back here." The man was red in the face and perspiring. He took a handkerchief from his pants and wiped at his brow. "My deer's heavier'n I figured. I hauled him to the edge of the field there. Figure I can back my car down. That's what I come back to ask you."

"Maybe I can help you bring it closer," said Joseph. "Up near here." He was trying to plan it all in his head. Now that the man had seen the beginnings of the deer's grave, it would not be so easy. Still, he could say he saw four or five boys tramp through the yard. When the man spoke again, Joseph began to feel better about it. The man said he thought he ought to find a place where he could grab a beer and a sandwich, since it was lunch time. Would it be all right if he left the deer for a longer time? Joseph agreed. It would make everything more feasible.

Then Joseph and the man began walking towards the edge of the field. The man was thanking Joseph for helping him; thanking him between huffs and puffs, so badly winded he was. When the man said, "There's my baby!" Joseph saw the deer. The dead eyes of the animal were staring up at him in the same frozen way *why?* of Ishmael; the mouth of the animal was cut, and the side of his face crushed in.

"Nobody gonna frame this baby over his fireplace," said the man. "I had to stun him. Telling you, he was a toughie! Legs kicking all over the place, and full of shot already. You can lift him from that end, if you don't mind."

Joseph knelt by the animal. He had his back turned on the hunter. He felt tears start to sting his eyes.

"Okay, now, can you lift him?"

Mechanically, Joseph grabbed the ropes. He began to move. The dead animal was heavy. He wondered at the fact the man had managed with him, even the short distance he had brought him from the woods. What makes a man want this dead, battered trophy that badly? Ugly Billy Duncan, the deer he had killed and beaten still more beautiful than ugly Billy Duncan, more beautiful than any thought ugly Billy Duncan would ever have, than any thing ugly Billy Duncan would ever make, than any part of ugly Billy Duncan who called the beauty his now. His!

They set the deer down by the barn.

"Wooooo, eee! That was a job!" said the man. He threw a coil of rope on the deer's body and took out his handkerchief again to wipe his face.

Joseph stared down at the deer. The deer's eyes fixed his. *Why?* Joseph looked at the rope. With the rope he could tie the deer behind the barn door under the burlap, just in case the man insisted on looking in the barn. He picked up the rope. The man was looking at one of Joseph's signs on the barn's side, under the POSTED sign. He was walking up to it now, his lips moving while he read it.

He turned, grinning. "Who wrote the poem? You?"

"Walter de la Mare wrote it," Joseph said.

"S'pretty good!"

Joseph stared at him. "What?"

"I said I like the poem. I don't like poems usually, you know? I like this one. 'Hi, handsome hunting man! Fire your little gun!' I don't know. It's got a certain rhythm, yah know?" Slowly, Joseph realized the man did not understand the poem. He watched him while he read it through again, heard him repeat: " '. . . peep again, creep again, leap again, eat or drink or sleep again—oh, what fun!' Yeah," he said, turning back to face Joseph again, "it's good!"

Joseph said, "You don't know what it means, do you?"

"It's about hunting. What do you mean, what it means?" He laughed, showing his row of corn. "I mean, it's obvious, ain't it?"

"Why do you think it's under a posted sign?" said Joseph.

"I suppose you're some kind of joker. Hell, I don't know. I leave the philosophy to my wife."

"You shouldn't," Joseph said. "Not this philosophy. It isn't for your wife. And I'm not a joker. I'm serious about that sign."

"The poem?" The man looked at him, a guarded expression on his face now. He was beginning to wonder about Joseph and it showed.

Joseph said, "What's good about an animal never leaping again, or sleeping, or eating? What's good about that?"

"We all gotta die some day," the man said. "I mean, well, the poem's like a rhyme. It's got a rhyme. I like it, that's all. Am I supposed to hate it? I like it!"

"You're stupid!" Joseph said. "You're stupid, *Billy*!"

"Hey now, just don't get wise, Mister. I mean, just don't!"

But Joseph could not stop himself now. He began walking towards the man slowly. "Stupid!" he was saying. "Too stupid to do anything but kill things more beautiful than one fracture of a second of your ugly life! Stupid! Stupid!"

Then the man took a swing at him, knocking Joseph back against the barn. Joseph felt his head throb with the pain of the impact. It was the first time in his life he had been hit by anyone but his father; the first time in his adult life that he had ever been hit by anyone. He looked at the man, and the man was shaking his head as though he were sorry for what he had done. Then the man walked towards him. "I shouldn't ah lost my temper like that. I don't like being called stupid, Mister," he was saying as he came towards Joseph. "I guess you got a right to your own opinions about me, coming here on your place a stranger, but I don't like anyone calling me—"

"Stupid!" Joseph finished the sentence for him. With a strength completely unknown to himself, Joseph had managed to catch the rope in his hand over the man's head. Now he was simply pulling. Pulling and waiting to see if Billy Duncan would ask *why?* too.

Chapter Thirteen

All the cards were on the table.

The table was a side one in the back of Michael's Pub. Maggie usually ate at Rattazzi's down the street, having switched from here to there a few years ago along with the rest of her crowd, but today Maggie wanted to lunch with Janice uninterrupted by the usual back-and-forth greetings. Driving in from Bucks County with Janice she had planned it this way—a few martinis to loosen the tongue, then spill!

"No," Janice Hart said, "I just can't imagine Lou purposely killing a cat. I'm not saying he didn't do it, Mag. I'm simply admitting there's a lot about Lou I don't understand."

"That Tondley business must have been awful for him!"

"Awful!"

"Then Joseph buying that goddamned book! If Lou had only looked inside! He couldn't have—else he would have known it was our cat he killed then. You see, Janice, he *couldn't* have known it was our cat he killed that night."

"A Sunday night, Hmmmm?"

"Yes."

"I wish I could remember which Sunday. Our days are all alike to me. Sunday—Sunday—A few weeks back."

"The whole thing's so goddamned ironical! Lou thinking Joseph knew that Tondley boy. Dear God! Look, let's have another drink"

"You see, Maggie," Janice said when the third whisky sour was put before her, "Lou's not easy to figure out. He thinks he's very uncomplicated, but he's just the opposite. He sets out to be a simple country doctor like his father, but you can fool some of the people only some of the time, and Lou didn't fool anybody. He wasn't simple and he wasn't country. Here comes the shirts from Brooks Brothers in the mail. Here come the cases and cases of seven-dollar Scotch. Since when does a country doctor read Leonard Lyons' column and grab the theatre section of the Sunday Times the first thing the paper gets in the house? Then, there's the place we live in. Dud Clymer was a wealthy man, Maggie. You know, red hunting coats and off to get the fox with other people in red hunting coats, that sort of thing. Since I can remember, it was Lou's dream to own the Clymer place. Well, we own it now! *And* a Mercedes Benz—and we owe 5,000 dollars and we're going to owe a hell of a lot more before Lou's done."

"Did he ever want to be anything but a doctor?"

"Never. There you are. You explain it."

"Well, he's compensating for something, Jan. I mean, that's what it is—compensation. Now, if he started all this *after* the Tondley business, I might understand it, but if he's always been this way—"

"Always. Only *after* Freddy Tondley died, he started living in the past. We could go into the back-number magazine business tomorrow!"

"I just don't get it!" Maggie said. "There's a lot of pent-up hostility there, that's easy enough. I mean, the Tondley thing, and going after cats, and—"

Janice Hart said, "Maggie, in all fairness to Lou, I have to say I don't think he went after your cat. I just can't believe it wasn't an accident."

"You saw him kick your dog, with your own eyes, Janice."

"Yes—yes, I saw that. Honestly, though, he's never done anything like that before this."

"And the Tondley thing," Maggie said. She paused a moment, being careful to put it the right way, "that *could* have been an unconscious hostility. Now, wait a minute, I'm not saying that Lou consciously wanted such a result, but he may have—"

Janice interrupted her. "Maggie, Lou was drunk when the call came. That's all. He didn't get the call and *then* start drinking. He was already so drunk he didn't even know he was taking the call."

"Ah!" Maggie said, "but he *did* know. Somewhere in his consciousness he knew enough to get in that car and head towards the Tondleys'! Look, Janny, I don't want to hurt you. God knows!"

"I know you don't."

"I just think you've got a bigger problem on your hands than you know."

"Yes. Yes, I can see that."

"You'd better get him to a doctor," Maggie said. "I'm saying this for your own good, Jan. I mean, for your good *and* Lou's."

"An analyst, hmmm. Oh, Mag, he'd just blow up if I suggested that."

"I'd risk it, believe me! Sometimes I think Joseph could use a little psychoanalyzing himself. The trouble is, Joseph doesn't want help. Lou is crying for it, Jan. That's what all the drinking means. He's begging for help. But Joseph—well, I'm afraid Joseph is just an out-and-out eccentric! He never was like anyone else and he never will be, that's all!"

"But you love him anyway, hmmm?"

"Joseph needs me, Jan. Pure and simple. Oh, *he* doesn't think so, but believe me, honey, that man needs me! I have to be needed! It's what makes me tick! I'm needed at A. & F. too. That's why I'm good, because A. & F. needs me."

"Lord!" Janice said, "Joseph must just hate us!"

"Not *you*, honey. Lou! That cat was like Joseph's child. You know, I used to be jealous of that cat? Jealous!"

"Is there anything we could do to make it up to him? Another cat, maybe? I know Lou will want to do something. I just know he doesn't even remember killing the cat, Maggie."

"Honey, all Lou needs to do is apologize to Joseph. Joseph really has a soft spot. He'll melt," Maggie snapped her fingers, "like that!"

"Lou will be sick about it. I mean that, Maggie."

"If he tells Joseph that, the whole thing will blow over. You know, Jan, in some ways they're very much alike."

"Except Joseph doesn't drink."

"No, well, he has other ways of compensating for his disappointments."

"But not bad ways."

"Not really. Nutty ways. The cat, for one thing. Joseph has his little world he lives in, just like Lou. The difference is, Joseph has control over his little world, and Lou doesn't. That's why I don't worry about Joseph."

"And you say Lou was really violent at your place Saturday morning"

"Not *really* violent. Now that I know the whole story, I can appreciate his mood. He's just suffering from a guilty conscience because of that Tondley boy."

"You don't really think Lou has unconscious hostility, do you, Maggie?"

"Honey, don't make it sound like a contagious disease. We all have it in varying degrees."

"I wish I could understand things the way you do, Maggie."

Maggie said, "Psychoanalysis gives you a sixth sense, Janny; that's all there is to it. Before I was analysed, *I* was married to a drinker. Nothing now and then about *his* drunks, either. He was preserved in alcohol. Never had a hangover in his life, for the simple reason he never sobered up. Well, *he* needed me too. Until he died at age thirty-three."

"I'm sorry, Mag. I had no idea you were married before."

"Oh yes, poor old Larry had problems. Big ones! He was a twin. Try living with a twin some time! His brother was a big-deal scholar, always scrounging around England to discover who wrote Shakespeare's plays and what was the origin of the Picts. Larry could barely grasp Longfellow." Maggie said, "Come on, let's have one more drink," and she signalled to the waiter. "So Larry drank, because dear old Luther was winning all the ribbons! I went through hell, Jan! Hell! Joseph may be an odd animal, but at least he's a tame one. It's the untamed ones you have to beware of, Janny."

"Like Lou?"

Maggie nodded. "I'm afraid so, honey."

Well, *someone* had to sound the alarm before it was too late.

2

As a finishing touch, Joseph turned the hunter's head so that his face was looking into the face of the deer beside him. It was strange that the animal's eyes seemed to be inquiring for an answer to the fatal injury, and the man's eyes demanded an answer to the fatal insult. It was as though the deer knew all along there would be an ending, and asked only why it was now and what had justified it—but the man seemed unable to fathom the fact his ending was possible. Between them was the gun. Now all that was left to do was cover over Billy Duncan and his deer.

Afterwards, Joseph spent hours piling leaves on top the dirt, then moving the woodpile from the side of the barn to the back, covering the leaves and the dirt with tall, neat stacks of logs. Maggie had often remarked that the wind swept across their property from the south. In the winter, it would cause huge drifts. The woodpile was better protected from the wind behind the barn; tomorrow Joseph would erect a small shelter over it. That night at dinner he would tell Maggie he had finally found a way to shelter their wood supply, and that he was working on it. Maggie would only half-hear, the way she always took in trivia, but if anything should come up in the future (what could?) the moving of the woodpile would not be at all suspect.

All the while Joseph was working on the woodpile, the classic quotations about murder ran through his head. Most of them had been copied from Chaucer's original statement in *The Canterbury Tales*: "Mordre wol out, certeyn, it wol nat faille."

Cervantes simply lifted it for *Don Quixote*: "Murder will out."

Then there was John Webster's *Dutchess of Malfi* with: "Murder shrieks out."

Then *Hamlet*: "Murder, though it has no tongue, will speak with most miraculous organ."

Joseph thought of four or five more versions, ending up with the more watered-down ones which simply promised, *Merchant-of-Venice* style: "Murder cannot be hid long."

He was calm while he mused over this and carefully stacked the logs, and when his memory had exhausted all the quotations, he fell to speculating about other murderers. Did they feel as he did now? Not hysterical, not numb either, but matter-of-fact. Literature had no answer to that question. Murderers were not writing literature, after all; they were murdering. A man who wrote a book could only imagine how a murderer might feel. Joseph had read scenes in mystery books where the murderer plunged a knife in a body over and over in some sort of crazy frenzy. What did the author know? Perhaps the murderer had plunged the knife in, noticed quite objectively how the blood trickled to the left, then plunged the knife in so as to make the next spurt of blood connect with the blood trickling from the left. Make a sort of pattern. Watch it a while, then another plunge, a new shape to the pattern. Couldn't it be that way just as well? Was it a violent thing, the feeling of murdering, or was it a graceful amusement? Murderers were not all cut from the same cloth, were they? Were they all mad, and was Joseph mad right now, carrying logs to cover the grave of a man and a deer, wondering if he were mad?

Joseph could not remember anything about the actual performance of the murder. It was a typical disaster reaction. He had read once in a study of disaster that the greater the incident, the less one perceived about it. A man could go to his death remembering another man slapping his face, but he would very likely not be able at all to remember being blown out of his apartment by an explosion in the boiler room.

Neither could Joseph remember why he had murdered Billy Duncan. He was ugly and stupid and he had brought a slain deer onto Joseph's property with Joseph's permission; was that a reason? Meaningless—the whole thing. How could he react to something absolutely meaningless? The answer was, he could not. He was perspiring, but he was doing hard work, and his heart was quieter than it often felt nights when he was reading alone in his study, and actually heard the beat. Fear? What did he have to be afraid of? He had murdered the man in an absolutely isolated spot where he could not possibly be observed. He had no connection with the man, other than the theft of the man's pheasant last Friday, and he had told no one—not even Maggie—about that. Guilt? No, why should there be any? The man meant nothing to him. Whoever it was waiting at home for Billy Duncan would surely feel nothing but relief at the eventual knowledge he would not be returning. Joseph only had to remember the pockmarks and the row of corn to believe that. He had probably done some poor woman a tremendous favour.

She would collect Billy's insurance and go on about the business of life, and better luck next time, Joseph thought. Even murder could not blight Billy Duncan's supposed end. One would either guess he was the victim of a shooting accident, or that he was one of these peculiar missing people, who seemed to just disappear into thin air. Like Judge Crater, or the West Point cadet—one of those. Years from now Joseph might well pick up a newspaper and see a "What happened to Billy Duncan?" article some hack might put together from old news clips, for a cheque to buy groceries.

The pity, to Joseph's way of thinking that Monday afternoon, was that he had never set his cap for this accomplishment: the perfect murder. Here it was, what some poor fellows exhausted all their energy trying to do, and Joseph had done it without a second's planning.

It was iron:cal, wasn't it, that three days ago about this time Joseph was carrying around a book called *The Unknown Murderer*? Now, he *was* the unknown murderer! Joseph gave a little chuckle. He felt gay. He felt very, very gay!

3

He woke up at ten minutes to six, in the dark of the bedroom. His sleep had been irregular, the fitful sort when one is too warm, too tired, and too preoccupied with wide-awake worries. The constant ringing of the phone had bothered it (the phone-answering service was usually careless, so that there were often eight and nine rings) and from downstairs there was the intermittent sound of Stilt's nervous-and-lonely howling. He was dressed in his clothes; he had not even bothered to remove his shoes. He was atop the chintz spread, with the lemon-shaded comforter pulled over him. Unshaven, and the sick-making taste of whisky and cigarettes in his mouth.

When he turned on the light, he saw Janice's note to him, on the floor. He had crumpled it up and tossed it there some time around noon, when he had arrived home. Now he bent over and straightened it out and reread it:

119

"I am going to New York for the day with Maggie Meaker. Dr. Ingram called. So did many patients of course, in person and via phone. Stilt has been fed."

Again he glanced at his wrist watch, calculating now whether or not it would be a good time to call Ingram. Today was Lou's hospital day. When he left Trenton early this morning, he had planned to report at the hospital; planned to go home first for a change of clothes and something to eat, then drive back to New Hope by ten. It was important to him because of Ingram. The old man had put a lot of trust in Lou when no one else would; Lou knew the old man counted on him not to be let down. He would have made it all right, if it had not been for the accident in Washington Crossing. It was not too serious, no one else was involved, but it had curled the left front fender of the Benz, and thrown the horn wires out of whack so that the horn blew for close to twenty minutes before Lou figured out a way of stopping it. He had hit a tree, turning too sharply on a curve. He supposed he had probably been still slightly drunk; there was no other explanation. It was the first time he had ever done damage to the car; and it was the last thing left for him to damage.

He cleared his throat a few times and said "Hello" a few times, to get the huskiness out of his voice; and then he reached for the phone. Ingram would be home about this time. He dialled the number, deciding the best way was simply to say he had been unavoidably detained; no apologies, no explanations. Either Ingram had called very early that morning, or Janice had left for New York very late. There was the possibility Ingram was not calling Lou about his absence at all. But when Ingram answered and recognized Lou's voice, his tone was unmistakably one of anger.

Lou started to say, "I was called to Trenton early this morning and it took me longer than—"

But the old man cut him off in the middle of the sentence. "Louis, you know Mrs. Glover-Hadley, I think?"

"Yes, of course. She has something to do with the hospital's board of directors."

"Not *something* to do with them, no. *Everything* to do

with them, Louis. You might say she *is* the board of directors. And you know her son, T. W.?"

"I don't *know* him."

"That isn't important, Louis. He knows you. He was over in Danboro Friday night. He told his mother you were there, intoxicated, and involved in a fist fight of some sort. No, don't say anything. Let me finish. She woke me up Saturday morning, calling me on the telephone. She said either you break your affiliation with the hospital or she'll break hers."

"I see."

"I tried to call you Saturday *and* Sunday. Then I tried again this morning before I left the house. Apparently you didn't go to the hospital this morning anyway."

"No, sir."

"I'm sorry about this, Louis. I think Mrs. Glover-Hadley is a meddler, she always was, and I think T. W. is a worse old woman than she is, but I also think you have a little soul-searching to do. Does that sound pontifical?"

"No, it doesn't."

"Your father was my closest friend, Louis. If you'd like to come and have a talk with me, I'd be glad to arrange some free time. Maybe talking with me would just embarrass you, I don't know, but if you ever want to give it a try, Louis, I'm available."

"Thank you, Dr. Ingram."

"Good night, then. Take care of yourself, Louis."

"Good night," Lou said. He put the phone's arm back in its cradle. Then he put his palms to his face and wept.

Outside it was beginning to snow. The dented Benz was parked in the back, beside the strange green station wagon. A patient's car, Lou had guessed when he had arrived home that morning; it had probably broken down and had to be temporarily abandoned.

Chapter Fourteen

Monday, Amos Fenton had imagined that what took place between him and Maggie last Friday night would undoubtedly be resolved with some John O'Hara-type conversation.

He imagined that it would happen some time during the work day at A. & F.; that it would go something like this:

Maggie: I suppose you're thinking the same thing I am?
Amos: If you mean that our timing was way off, yes.
Maggie: Yes, something like that. Only I wasn't thinking it was our timing that was off. There'll never be a time, will there, Amos?
Amos: Friday was probably as close as we'll ever come to it.
Maggie: Are you sorry? I am.
Amos: I am, too.
Maggie: Then we just as good as, in a way.
Amos: Yes, I guess we just as good as. End of story.

But Monday produced neither that kind of talk, nor Maggie, and neither did Tuesday. Wednesday when Maggie missed work again Fenton began worrying. Maybe he had misjudged both Maggie *and* Joseph, and let himself in for something he was not in any mood to handle. He was already in up to his neck with the Waverly Soap people, a client that really did relate cleanliness to Godliness. Their latest gripe was over one of the girls who sang "The Waverly Wonderful" commercial. It seemed she had abandoned her illegitimate child when she was 19, and now was fighting in the courts for its return, with much "yellow newspaper" publicity. The newspapers were on her side, but the Waverly Soap people said her presence in the commercial would automatically associate the Waverly Soap baby with bastards—and somehow Amos Fenton was just as responsible as the man who had run out on the girl. Thursday Amos spent the day with the client convincing him he was God-fearing, his children were all legitimate, and by the time "Waverly Wonderful" was heard in the sticks, no one would remember that the girl third from the left had once forgotten herself. At nine o'clock that night, back in Greenwich, immersed in domesticity (a game of "Scrabble for Juniors" with his boys) the radio broadcast the news. The name Billy Duncan rang no bells, but Old Ferry Road did; so did the name Dr. Louis Hart. Friday morning just as Fenton was on the verge of suggesting Maggie have lunch with him, Maggie herself called for the same reason.

"Do you mind if we eat in? It's more private."

Amos Fenton understood perfectly.

"I tried to get hold of you yesterday," said Maggie when he shut the door behind him, shortly after noon.

"I was with old man Tuckerman from Waverly."

"Have you read the newspapers on this?"

"I only saw the *Times* this morning, but I heard something last night. Look, is it serious?"

"Read this, first," Maggie said. She handed him one of the morning sheets, the same one which was involved with a mercy plea for the girl in "Waverly Wonderful." There was a picture of a private in an Army uniform, carrying a gun with a bayonet fixed to it, and wearing a combat helmet. Beside that was a smaller, less focused snapshot of a man holding a fedora in his hand, an older version of the soldier. The older version was wearing a well-pressed suit, standing beside a station wagon, carrying a girl, about four, in his right arm. Fenton read the story.

MYSTERY SHROUDS HERO'S DISAPPEARANCE

"The disappearance of World War II hero William (Billy) Duncan, of Lambertville, New Jersey, is taking on a mysterious air, with Dr. Louis Hart's insistence that he and Duncan never met.

"Duncan, 42, has been missing since Monday morning. His wife, Muriel, told police her husband left for a hunting expedition in Bucks County, Pennsylvania, at seven-thirty that morning.

"Duncan's green station wagon was found parked behind the home of Dr. Louis Hart, on Old Ferry Road, in the rural district of New Hope.

"Hart's story is that he noticed the car when he

arrived home from a visit to Trenton, New Jersey, close to noon on Monday. Believing that it was a patient's car which might have broken down, he ignored the green station wagon until the following day. He then telephoned police to report that it was there, claiming that he knew no one named William Duncan.

"Reporters subsequently learned that Hart and a man answering Duncan's description were seen together at a Danboro bar last Friday evening. Dr. Hart was asked to leave the bar after a fight with the man.

"Something of a 'character' in rural New Hope, Dr. Louis Hart was cleared of a charge of 'negligence' some five years ago, when he failed to appear at the scene of a fatal accident, for which his professional services had been requested. The victim of the accident, involving an electric saw, died while Dr. Hart slept in his car, allegedly en route, until he pulled over to the side of the road for a nap.

"Hart has not been able to explain his whereabouts from Friday until late Monday morning to the satisfaction of the investigating police.

"Meanwhile, where is Billy Duncan? A battle-tried veteran of World War II, hero in the invasion of Sicily with the 47th Regiment, Duncan is a sturdy, crack-shot sportsman. The father of six children, he is a salesman for the Merriweather Mayonnaise Corporation, of Merriweather, Pennsylvania.

"His wife told reporters she is sure her husband does not know Dr. Louis Hart. She cannot explain how her husband's car came to be parked behind the Hart house, unless he had been involved in an accident of some sort, and gone there for medical aid.

"Alfred White, bartender at the Danboro Bar, identified Duncan from photographs. He claims Duncan and the doctor met at the bar, and had a fight about the doctor's drinking. This was Friday night. Duncan returned to Lambertville and spent Saturday and Sunday with his family.

"Where was Hart during that time?

"Where is Duncan now?"

Fenton put the newspaper back on Maggie's desk.

"I suppose *we're* going to be involved?"

"Not if we can help it, and not just to save our own necks either, Amos."

"Well, that's what *I'm* interested in, frankly. Saving *our* necks. This could get out of hand, Maggie. You know damn well! We saw Hart *after* he left Danboro. There was a fight! What was the fight about? Hell, you know yourself—"

"Wait, just *wait*! I spent all day Wednesday with Janice Hart. Lou doesn't remember anything, naturally. We filled him in on what we could. By the way, he sent his apologies."

"Thanks."

"He's really not a bad guy, Amos. I feel damn sorry for him."

"Okay."

"We all agree there is absolutely no point in mentioning his visit with us. He went from Danboro to Trenton, checked in at some motel, and stayed there. He can prove that. He's done it before too, so it's nothing suspicious. He's just going to have to say he drinks, and when he drinks, he does that."

"Okay. But what's the truth?"

"That's the truth! He was at some motel the whole weekend. Jan called me about it Saturday and again Sunday. That's the way he is, that's all."

"What about this guy Duncan?"

"Well, he probably did have a fight with him. He claims he doesn't remember, but the next day he had some bruises."

"Hell, that could have been my fist's work! I don't get it! Couldn't he explain it better if he just said *we* had a fight? I'm not suggesting that, of course, God knows! I don't want any connection with this thing. But I don't get *his* reasoning."

Maggie lit a cigarette. "Listen carefully, Amos. Lou Hart claims that if Alfred White says Lou was fighting with someone in his bar, Alfred White is telling the truth. Lou says the fellow doesn't lie. All right. So suppose he met this Duncan and fought with him, and there are witnesses apparently. No, never mind the apparently. There *are* witnesses. Okay, then he left Danboro and came to our house. Why? Don't you see? We'd just make it all worse for him. And for ourselves! The police would want to know why he didn't go home afterwards and what he did while he was there, and there's just no point in making him look any more unstable than he already looks to everyone."

"I'm for that, all right. I don't want to have anything to do with it."

"That's exactly what Lou says. He doesn't want us involved either."

"How does *he* explain Duncan's car being at his place?"

"He can't explain it. He's a mess!"

"How do you explain it, Maggie? You look like you're holding out on me."

"I think the same thing his wife thinks, that he had an accident or something and saw the doctor's sign. Believe me, Janice and I left for New York together about eight. There was no green station wagon at the place then. Why couldn't he have had an accident in the woods nearby and then driven to the Harts'?"

"He could have. It's logical. But where is he now?"

"I don't know. I just don't know."

"What do you know about this fellow Hart, I mean, *really*?"

"Not a lot, Amos. Not anything."

"What about this case of negligence?"

"He's a drinker. He was soused when he got the call, and passed out before he could get there. Oh, he doesn't deserve any medals of any kind, but——"

"But what?"

"I just don't think he murdered this Duncan fellow."

"Who said he did?"

"Well, you know damn well that's what the newspapers are implying!"

"Anything else, Maggie? I can tell there's more."

"Yes, there's more. While he stayed at the motel in Trenton he registered under the name Duncan Tondley."

Amos Fenton whistled. "*Duncan* Tondley! Nice! Where'd he get the *Duncan* from? How's he going to explain that? How do you explain it, for that matter?"

"I think he did meet this Duncan fellow, and they did have a fight. He was blotto, you know that yourself; he was looped, Amos! Well, he remembered the Duncan in his unconscious mind. That explains the Duncan. There's a small matter of the Tondley, though, which I can't explain, not unless you give me a lot of time, and a martini."

"Tondley? Didn't he use that name Friday night at your place too?"

"Freddy Tondley was the name of the electric-saw victim in the negligence case! Yes, he was yelling it around Friday night."

"For God's sake! Maggie, are you going to sit there and say that two and two makes accident? Tondley was the guy he let die! Duncan Tondley! You said something about time and a martini explaining everything. I suppose he's a Jekyll-Hyde. You going to tell me that? Duncan Tondley! Maggie, is it sinking in on you at all? This sounds like one hell of a goddam juicy scandal. Murder, and no kidding!"

"I know how it *sounds*! But I can explain the 'Tondley.' We have to begin way back, Amos, with Joseph's Siamese and a certain cat-hater who's a mechanic at the New Hope garage. Are you ready to adjourn to a dark, private corner, say, *upstairs* in that French place across the street? I'm out of the mood for ordering up."

"Lord knows, *I* could use a drink."

"You should see Joseph," Maggie said, pulling her pocketbook out of her desk drawer. "You wouldn't know him any more."

"I never did."

"Well, even so. You'd see the difference in him. You'll understand better when I tell you the whole story."

"You mean Joseph's mixed up in it?"

"Let's say, he *thinks* he is. Well, he's right too, in a way. But he's not responsible for whatever happened to this Duncan. That's what he can't get through his head. So—he's drinking."

"Good for him! That's what I'd do."

"It's not the drinking, Amos. Not just the drinking! It's the change that comes over him when he drinks!"

"What is he, violent or something? Abusive?"

"Dear old Amos," Maggie said crossing the room, straightening Fenton's tie, "dear old Maggie, for that matter! We're logical folk, that's our trouble. If someone like Joseph were to drink, someone like Joseph would become violent and abusive, that's the way we think. Well, the Josephs in the world are a little more complicated than that! Do you want to stop upstairs for your topcoat?"

"No." He opened the door of her office for her. "Well, what about Joseph when he drinks?"

"He's happy," Maggie said, "he's happy as a lark!"

2

Friday morning only one patient showed up at Lou Hart's, an old woman suffering with giardiasis. Lou wrote out a prescription for Atabrine dihydrochloride and gave it to her, and she said she was sorry about all the trouble he was in.

"That Duncan fellow's probably out in the woods with a bullet in his head," she said. "Some hunter probably mistook him for an animal, Doctor, now that's what I think."

"You take these three times daily, five or six days," Lou told her, "and if you have any upset, you take some sodium bicarbonate. I'll give you some samples I have here."

She smiled and said, of course that did *not* explain how Duncan's car got in his drive, "but he could have just parked it there now, couldn't he, Doctor Hart? Just figured you were a doctor and one car more or less in your drive wouldn't go noticed, now that's what I think."

"Thank you, Mrs. Sussman," said Lou. "I hope you feel better."

"Is poor Mrs. Hart all upset, Doctor?"

"No," Lou lied. "Now, you let me know how you feel."

"And Tony? How's little Tony?"

"He'll be home for the holidays," said Lou.

"All the way from Paris, France?"

"Yes," Lou said. "For Christmas."

"Coming all the way across the ocean, hmmm? Looks bad, don't it?"

128

"He was coming home for the holidays, anyway," Lou
lied again.

"Well, don't you worry, Doctor. Plenty of us around
here think the world and all of you, no matter what."

This time Lou was able to get her coat on her, and
propel her towards the door. She would pray for him, she
said.

As he held open the door for her, he saw Captain Plant
from the State Police Barracks, waiting down the hall in
the reception room. Mrs. Sussman's eyes followed Lou's,
and she sucked in her breath with a little s-s-s-s noise and
crept down the hall as though she were in danger of being
arrested herself.

Lou called out a "Come in, Captain," and Plant put
down a copy of *Look* magazine and lumbered towards
Lou. He was a big man, wearing his official uniform
complete with boots, and smoking a Cigarillo. Lou and he
had known one another close to ten years; Plant's
daughter was Tony's age. Up until this moment, other
officers from the State Barracks had talked with Lou; this
was Plant's first appearance. He went through the usual
amenities, then said abruptly, "Well, what have we got
here, Lou?"

"As far as I know you have a missing person."

"Yes. You never met Billy Duncan?"

"I don't remember meeting him, Jack. I guess I did,
though, a week ago tonight."

"Alfred White says so, and T. W. Glover-Hadley says
so, and a few others hanging around in Danboro. Then we
got this report from The Washington Crossing Motel, near
Trenton. You registered there as *Duncan* Tondley.
Right?"

"Yes."

"You want to tell me about that?"

"The 'Duncan' was probably because I met this fellow
Duncan, and his name stuck. The 'Tondley'—well, I
suppose it's *engraved* on my unconscious. I suppose I still
feel guilty about it. I just put the two names together
somehow."

"You didn't feel guilty about Duncan too, for some
reason?"

"Jack, I don't know. I don't remember! I'm probably implicating myself all to hell with this kind of admission, but that's the truth. I don't remember meeting Duncan. I don't remember fighting with him. I don't remember signing his first name on the motel slip. I don't remember ever seeing his car before Monday noon, and his photographs don't ring any bells."

"You were going at it pretty heavy, hmmm?"

"That's right."

"Any particular reason?"

"A drunk doesn't need a reason, I guess."

"I'm sorry about this, Lou, but it doesn't look good for you."

"Let me ask you the same question you asked me, Jack. What do you think we've got here?"

"Well, I don't think it's a missing person. I think it's a dead person. Billy Duncan's been missing five days now. He's not in the woods, we've combed the woods, and he's not anywhere else. I'd say we got homicide here, murder or manslaughter—your guess is as good as mine; at least I don't *think* it's any better than mine."

"Homicide without a body, and I'm a suspect, is that it?"

"Yes."

"What happens to me?"

"Oh, I could arrest you on suspicion of murder, but you wouldn't be convicted without the body. What happens to you? I guess time will tell. The body will turn up; then time will tell."

"I see."

"Meanwhile, questions. Lots of questions."

"Yes."

"Are you busy tomorrow morning, for example?"

"Would it make any difference?"

"Oh, we'd fit it in with your schedule. It's not that bad yet. *Mrs.* Duncan's coming over tomorrow around noon. Could you be there then?"

"At the Barracks?"

"Yes."

"All right, Jack."

"We could be all wrong, Lou," Captain Plant said getting up. He stubbed out his Cigarillo in Lou's ashtray.

"I'm not a heavy drinker myself. Maybe I drink a bottle of whisky over a period of two months. I don't know anything about these blackouts. I *do* know if I were in your shoes, Lou, I'd put on my thinking cap. Try to remember something. Hell, I don't think you'd hurt a fly, intentionally. I just don't! But then again, Billy Duncan wasn't a fly, and neither was Freddy Tondley. I'm sorry, but it looks lousy."

"Tomorrow around noon," Lou said.

Chapter Fifteen

During those five days, Joseph read "thrillers." He bought them at the news-store in Doylestown, paperbacks which he read at the rate of five or six a day. Now that he was a murderer, it interested him to see how close an author could come to imagining how he felt, or to creating a murder scene in any way similar to last Monday's scrimmage out behind the barn.

He was sorely disappointed. Like love scenes in novels, murder scenes in mysteries more than often portrayed the hero as slightly tipsy. Only in cases of murder for financial gain or through passion or husbands trying to exterminate their wives did the hero seem to go on his own power. Even in some of those, the murder scene was preceded by one of whisky-drinking.

Joseph began to think of these sodden villains as "outside men." They were nice guys until they drank; and when they were not nice guys, they were at least passing as nice guys; but drink did it. Joseph thought of all the "outside men" pouring liquor down their throats into the mouths of little "inside men." Then the insiders grew bigger and stronger and ultimately powerful enough to overtake their benefactors. They would emerge, murder, and shrink back inside; some to die there, some to stay docile and undemanding until the next heavy supply of kill-energy.

From there Joseph went to the possibility of "inside men." Wasn't that what he had always been? Holding himself back always? Varda had told him he kept his thoughts in "the big bottle," never mind Maggie's never-ending lectures on his over-control! He was an "inside man," and by staying so inside of himself, he had forced himself out. Now, to force himself back in again, he must stay outside. Drink might do it, he thought, and when Maggie came home nights, Joseph began having three or four martinis before dinner. The first night —Monday—Maggie had said things between them were the way she had always dreamed they might be. Joseph had regaled Maggie with stories of the strange hill called the Hexenkopf, in Northampton County, ten miles north of Haycock Mountain. The name meant Witch's Head, and the neighbourhood abounded with hexerei and stories of witches' doings. Joseph told her about the short life span of trees on the Hexenkopf, and of the holes in the ground near the dying ones, said to have been "stung" by hoopsnakes, who rolled up and down the Hexenkopf. He told her of the fruits of the Hexenkopf, more bitter and strange tasting than the same fruits grown in Haycock or Buckwampum, and he told her of the strange lights on the old hill, the punky wood of old tree stumps glowing with phosphorescence. Joseph walked about while he told her these things, his cheeks burning with the warmth of the gin, his glass raised in his hand, his voice loud and confident; and Maggie actually laughed at the way he made some of the stories so spooky—and afterwards, when she was asleep, he smoked a cigarette in his study and read a poem from the Varda file, shed a tear and smiled and felt a tenderness towards life.

He liked being an "outside man." He wished that all the other Josephs everywhere were just a little bit high, as he was. It wouldn't do them any good to keep holding everything in that way; he wished there were some way he could tell them that.

The next morning he had a hangover. He did not get up to have breakfast with Maggie, and when he breakfasted by himself, he felt sullen. He thought of Billy Duncan's ugly face and he was glad he had killed him. When Louis called shortly after one in the afternoon, and explained that it was a garage mechanic who had killed Ishmael, he thanked Louis very solemnly for the information and hung up without the predictable exchange of "I'm sorry I thought it was you" and "I can see how you would think it was me" and the rest of the apologies. He realized he could not even recall one of the little, lovely memories of the cat, which had been both a comfort and a pain to him in the days since the death of his pet. He felt nothing. Was that it? Once the "inside man" like Joseph lets go, an apathy is released with the violence. "I don't care," Joseph said aloud. His own voice sounded like a stranger's.

That day he read the usual amount of "thrillers" and some of the greats who wrote about murder as well. The

Greeks, and dreary, moralizing Shakespeare, then Eliot. Then he found "Fragment of an Agon," and he could not stop rereading it. There were marvellous lines like:

> "I knew a man once did a girl in,
> Any man has to, needs to, wants to
> Once in a lifetime, do a girl in."

In a way, he envied that murderer. A crime of passion, probably. Classic! Not low, like his. Not with a Billy Duncan for a victim! A Billy Duncan was not good enough for murder. He should have been run over by a bus, or drowned in the children's section of some community centre pool, attempting "the crawl."

Still, the poem was good; it said it best! Joseph walked about the house saying some of the poem's lines aloud, changing "girl" to man in the verse, reciting it while he made another pot of coffee for his headache: "I knew a man once did a man in."

Carrying the coffee over to the kitchen table, he paused to look in the mirror by the coat rack. His reflection was matter-of-fact as he recited:

> "I gotta use words when I talk to you
> But if you understand or if you don't
> That's nothing to me and nothing to you
> We all gotta do what we gotta do."

That was right. We all have to do what we have to do.

Tuesday night he was gay with gin again.

He had this conversation with Maggie:

"What made you suddenly take up drinking, Joseph?"

"Oh, it was high time. High time!"

"Was it because of what I told you Monday night? About Louis Hart and the Tondley boy?"

"No, Maggie dear, it was just as I said. High time!"

"It *was* because of that. You feel guilty about giving Louis that book. Now it's worse, because you know he didn't even kill Ishmael."

"Worse? You said yourself, last night, that things were fine between us. That things were the way you'd dreamed they'd be! Maggie, remember saying that last night?"

"Yes, yes, I remember. But things are serious for Louis, Joseph. You know that. I think you feel partially to blame, that's the reason for this false euphoria."

"Spinoza said: 'He who would distinguish the true from the false must have an adequate idea of what is true and false."

"Never mind Spinoza, Joseph, that's your fourth martini you're pouring."

Joseph said, "We all gotta do what we gotta do."

Later that night Maggie drove to the Harts. She suggested that Joseph come along. When he refused, she said she could understand his embarrassment, but he would have to face Lou Hart one day, he may as well get used to that idea. Joseph chuckled over that thought while he got out his paints. He was no longer interested in Louis Hart, not in the least bit interested in him. He knew exactly how stupid Billy Duncan's car had been left in Louis' driveway, the same way stupid Billy Duncan had wandered into Joseph's yard, by accident. Duncan was a blundering buffoon, the sort who left his hat under a seat at the theatre and walked off without it, or forgot which dry cleaner had his best suit. Dumb! Dumb Billy Duncan, little Billy dumb Duncan, lost his car at the doctor's house, lost his pheasant, his deer, his car, then his life—Joseph poured himself a little more gin and began to sketch the living room fireplace. Once, during college, he had played with the idea of being an artist. His sense of colour was excellent. Another student in his painting class had once mistaken one of Joseph's oils for a Henner—so long ago, everything so long ago. His shoulders and arms were very tired and the sketch was affected as a result. His shoulders and arms had ached ever since he had made Billy Duncan's grave. The fireplace looked like a huge mouth, open and waiting and insatiable. The mouth of the "inside man?" Across the page Joseph scribbled INSIDE OUT. He remembered an old silly poem by a woman with a silly name; what was her name? The poem was about the inner half of clouds being bright and shining—"I therefore. . . . I therefore. . . ." Then he remembered:

"I therefore turn my clouds about
And always wear them inside out
To show the lining."

By Ellen Thorneycroft Fowler. Ha!
That's what I'm doing, Joseph thought happily as he reached for his gin—wearing my clouds inside out.
Then Wednesday. Another hangover and the depressing announcement from Maggie that she was not going to work that day.
"You mean you're going to desert Picks Cigarettes and Risestaver Coffee and Amos Fenton?" said Joseph.
Maggie was pulling on her red gondolier pants from Bonwit's, while Joseph watched her from bed, feeling the same sullen way he had yesterday morning.
Maggie said, "You know, I don't think I like your new personality."
"Going to the Harts' again? A little Hart-to-Hart talk again today?"
"Joseph!" Maggie said, "whether you realize it or not things are in a mess! Last night you were too sleepy to listen, but it seems now that Lou *did* know this Billy Duncan!"
Then she told him the whole story, and Joseph listened as though someone were reading a story to him; as though he were not involved in any of it.
Maggie finished by saying, "It's crazy, but that's the way it is! The police are actually suspicious of Lou! Jan's so worried she's cabled Tony to come home."
"What has it all got to do with us, Maggie?" Joseph said.
"Oh my God, I wish you'd get analyzed!" Maggie shouted at him.
When she left the house Joseph wandered up to his study. He had been reading some more from the Varda file last night, had he? He leaned down and picked up a piece of yellowed paper from the floor where it had fallen. The poem "Dear"—he looked at it.
"Do I live at the fireplace of your eyes?"
He might just as well have chased around after Edgar Guest, he decided.
On his desk were his notes on hexerei, his paper on

sgraffito ware and the dissertation on *gruttafoos*. He opened the drawer to the right and pushed all of it in there; then shut it. From the drawer on the left, he took out a paperback novel from a pile of them stacked there. It was a Dashiell Hammett; he had marked his place with one of Maggie's hairpins. He sank into his comfortable chair and took up where he had left off: "God will see that there's always a mug there for your gun or blackjack to sock, a belly for your foot. . . ."

When Maggie came home near six that night, the martini pitcher was full, cooling in the refrigerator.

After his first drink, Joseph said, "I'm sorry about this morning. I was rude. I hope everything is all right at the Harts'! I really do!" And he meant it. He hoped everything was all right at the Amos Fentons', at the John Kennedys', at T. S. Eliots', at The Risestaver Coffee Corporation—everywhere, he hoped everything was all right. That afternoon in the *Bucks County Journal*, he had seen a picture of Billy Duncan's widow. She was sitting on one of those old-fashioned davenports, the kind with claw feet and antimacassars, and there were half a dozen assorted children climbing over her and the couch. She wore a shabby flowerprint housedress and rimless glasses. Muriel. He hoped everything was all right with Muriel too.

"Everything is *not* all right at the Harts', Joseph! Please don't pretend! You know very well what the situation is!"

"I guess I do. Better than anyone, really."

"You see, you *do* feel responsible! Look, Billy Duncan's fate—whatever it is—isn't *your* fault."

"Isn't it, Maggie?" Joseph smiled. "More martini?"

"No, thank you. And I wish you'd cut it out! Oh, I know how you feel, Joseph. It was simply a series of unfortunate coincidences, that's all."

"Wear your clouds inside out, Maggie dear," Joseph said.

"Lou doesn't even remember being here Friday. We've agreed to keep quiet about it. It won't help him."

"Remember when I used to have blackouts? Remember that was why I stopped drinking?"

"That's right. I thought of that today. Back on 94th Street you used to drink and go out and not remember where you were. I hope that's not going to start all over."

"No. Those were my salad days, Maggie. I was just a little out of control. But I soon brought myself to, didn't I, dear? I got a good hold on myself!"

"Then why lose it?"

"I don't have any reason for it any more, dear. Control implies there's something you have to hold in check. Well, there isn't any more."

"What do you mean, Joseph?"

"I'm wearing my clouds inside out!"

Maggie got very angry. "Oh, stop it!" she shouted at him. "Stop it! Stop it!"

Before they went to bed that night she asked him very seriously if he would consent to an interview with her psychoanalyst. Just as seriously, Joseph said he would not. He felt bad that she cried herself to sleep. From his study, he could hear her in there sobbing. He wondered if Muriel Duncan was sobbing herself to sleep as well. Then he remembered that day he was driving along the canal and he had seen the tall, lone Boy Scout, lagging behind the other smaller boys, slumped over with the handkerchief in his hand, bawling. Why had it not occurred to him to stop and go up to the boy, to help him? What kind of a person had he been before all this happened to him! And he thought of that night with Varda on the day of the Wallace rally; and he wanted to cry out to her as though she were a God who could hear and grant forgiveness for the way he had been, and not a girl who had married someone else and now no longer knew or cared that he was sorry. So long ago. And he had never thanked the boy in his art class who had mistaken his oil painting for a Henner. He had never said to him, "How proud you've made me!"; not said anything to him. God!

He shut his eyes, wet with tears, and remembered again those beloved words: ". . . and my dear I love your soul—profound, sad, wise and exalted like a symphony . . . !"

"Lies!" he screamed, "Lies, Varda!"

He woke up the next day there in his study. It was ten minutes after eleven and Maggie was gone. Scotch-taped to the bathroom mirror was a note from her:

Dear Joseph,
I don't know whether you realize how very drunk you were last night! I know you are troubled. I appreciate the fact it is hard for you to talk about it with me, much less admit it to yourself. I want to help you. I can't if you continue to shut me out.
You are perfectly right in reacting to this difficulty with seriousness, and *I* know it *is* seriousness, and not the frivolity you pretend to be taking it with. Lou Hart is in dire trouble. By accident, you had something to do with it. If you can just pull yourself together long enough to realize that the best way you can help him now is by getting yourself under control, it will be a very unselfish and fine thing to do. You have always been an overly-sensitive person. I should have appreciated that fact when I came home Monday night and blurted out all that Janice had told me about Lou, and I never should have hammered at you for giving him that book. I too have my selfish moments. I honestly did not realize how much you were going through inside that first night. . . . Now that I do, I beg you to let me help you, this once! Think about it through the day. Always, M.

After he shaved, he drove to Doylestown to buy the newspapers, and four or five more "thrillers." His stomach was queasy and he had a slight headache. When he came to the Cross Keys Diner on his way back from Doylestown, he went in for a coffee. He took the newspapers with him, and spread them before him in a back booth while he sipped the coffee. The *Times* was not giving the story very much space, and it was buried in the back pages, but the local papers were playing it up big, as were the Philadelphia papers. The *Doylestown Daily* had a photograph of Muriel, a different one from the picture in the *Bucks County Journal*. She was sitting in a rocking chair knitting, before a television set. She seemed very small and thin and unhappy, and over her photograph was the headline: "THE NIGHTS ARE LONG NOW . . ."
Under the picture was the story.

Tonight is Thursday. At eight-thirty, after the children are in bed, Muriel Duncan will walk into her small, cozy, front room on Landers Lane in Lambertville, New Jersey, and turn on the television. She will sit and knit on the red sweater she is making for her youngest boy, and watch "Bat Materson." She will watch "The Untouchables," and she will watch "The Million Dollar Movie." It will have seemed like any other Thursday night for Muriel Duncan, were it not for one fact. Her husband will not be there watching their favourite shows with her.

Tonight is Thursday, and Billy Duncan will not be home, not unless his wife's prayers are answered. He is not working late at the office, and he is not ill in the hospital, and he is not out of town on one of his frequent business trips as a salesman for the Merriweather Mayonnaise Corporation. "Please bring him back to me," Muriel Duncan prays each night. Back from where? Nobody knows. Back from a hunting trip he went on Monday morning, or back from the dead—nobody knows. The green station wagon which was found in the yard of Dr. Louis Hart, of New Hope R.D. No. 1, is once more back in the Duncan garage, but there is no trace of the man who set off in that car on the first day of deer season.

There are many mysterious rumours. Rumours of a fight between Billy and the doctor on last Friday night, in Danboro, Pennsylvania. Rumours of a "lost weekend" during which the doctor registered at a Trenton motel, under the name Duncan Tondley. Why "Duncan"? The doctor has no answer. Why "Tondley"? The answer to that question embarrasses the doctor. Five years ago Dr. Louis Hart was charged with negligence in the death of another war hero, Fredrick Tondley, victim of an electric-saw accident. The doctor was never able to explain fully why he said he would be there to aid Tondley, and then set off in his car only to pull to the side of the road and nap while Tondley was dying.

There are rumours, theories, and some plain old-fashioned hunches, but there is still no answer to the question: Where is Billy Duncan?

"When Billy was overseas in all that fighting and war," Mrs. Duncan said, "I somehow knew he'd get back to me. I don't have that feeling this time. The nights are long and I can't sleep wondering about it all."

"The Million Dollar Movie," then the news, and then?

Maybe another movie. The nights are long for Muriel Duncan.

Joseph folded up the paper, paid for his coffee and drove home. He read some of the paperbacks for a while, then he sat back deep in his chair and shut his eyes and thought for a while. In a way, he was sorry that Louis Hart had not been Ishmael's killer. It would all be poetic justice then. It was just messy now. If it had not been for the fact Louis had remembered that the Sunday night Ishmael was killed, a mechanic had driven his Benz, even Louis might be convinced he was both the cat's killer and Duncan's. A "blackout" killer—it would all at least have been more interesting that way.

As it was, it was shabby. Was the world really supposed to mourn over Muriel Duncan watching "Bat Masterson" alone on Thursday nights? Joseph sighed and went downstairs to the kitchen. Even though it was only three o'clock, he fixed himself a before-dinner martini.

By the time Maggie came home, he was very jolly, as usual, with the gin inside him. At the sound of her footsteps on the side porch, Joseph hurried to the door to greet her. Maggie was smiling, and in her arms she held a Siamese cat.

"Surprise, Joseph!"

It was not a kitten, but it was not yet a year old. It was badly frightened. When Joseph took it from Maggie's hands to hold it close, the cat squirmed and scratched and Maggie urged him to be careful with her. "Not too rough, Joseph!"

Joseph knew he was very high. He went about fixing up a bed by the fireplace for the cat, telling Maggie that he would name her Yillah, jumping about the kitchen and talking too fast, and all the time thinking he really only wanted to get everything over with so he could sit down and have his next drink. Maggie had several drinks with him, and that was what he liked, sitting there with the drinks and the talk; and when Maggie lit the candles and served a modest dinner of lamb chops and salad, Joseph picked at the food to please her, and talked and talked. He told Maggie that Yillah, in Melville's book *Mardi*, was a beautiful golden-haired girl who represented truth. Maggie seemed fascinated with his account of the book, with the stories of the heroes in *Mardi* who searched the world for Yillah. At one point Joseph became so excited with his recollections of the beautiful novel, that he stood up on his chair and recited: "Yillah! Yillah! now hunted again that sound through my soul. Oh, Yillah! too late, too late have I learned what thou art!"

"You really like the cat?" Maggie asked.

"Of course!"

He went to sleep very early, very drunk, and happy. Before he dropped off Maggie ran a cool hand across his brow. "It'll be all right now, Joseph," she said.

Friday morning when Joseph woke up, he did not remember the cat right away. He mixed himself a Bromo and shaved and dressed, trying to recollect a dream he had had about Muriel Duncan. Something about her glasses, about getting new frames for them. He was disgusted with himself for caring about the woman enough to dream of her. He opined that if he were to dream of anyone, it ought to be of Louis. It was Louis who was coming out the worst in the matter. Yet Louis, to Joseph's mind, was like some lost cause he had already wasted too much time on. Hating Louis had taken too much energy, too; and the knowledge that it was all for nothing, made Joseph even more tired of Louis Hart when he thought about him.

When he went downstairs, he saw the cat. She was sitting in the box he had made for her, by the fireplace. She was not a very handsome cat, scrawny and scared, with a fat face that was oddly out of proportion with the rest of her. Joseph remembered too that he had decided to call her Yillah. He did not know why he was annoyed with her presence in his house, but his hangover was too painful to dwell on the annoyance. He walked across and said, "Hello, Yillah," bent over to pick her up.

She spat at him and he pulled his hand away.

"Did I handle you too roughly last night, is that it?"

He put his finger by her chin and she bit him hard.

"All right, have it your way."

Joseph wandered across to the stove for coffee. On the counter-top was a note from Maggie, Scotch-taped to the toaster. He ran the water in the sink to get it good and cold for a drink, and read Maggie's message.

"Yillah (her name used to be Miss Me, so she may have trouble with the new one) is eight months old. Tom Spencer knew a neighbour who wanted to place her, so it's really a sort of premature Christmas gift from Tom and Miriam. The cat is used to the outdoors and likes mackerel. She's housebroken on newspapers, but prefers the outdoors! See you around six. So glad you like Yillah! Love, M.

"P.S. Weekend to ourselves!"

Joseph drank two full glasses of cold water and stood by the sink thinking of Maggie and Tom Spencer. "Give him a cat," he could imagine Tom Spencer advising, "something to take his mind off Ishmael and all the rest of it."

"Perfect!" Maggie had probably said, "but won't he think that's exactly what we're trying to do, and resent it a bit?"

"Oh," Tom Spencer undoubtedly countered, "tell him *I* got the cat from a neighbour, and it's sort of a premature Christmas gift from Miriam and me."

Joseph went back to the fireplace and stared down at the cat. She stared back, blue eyes like ice.

"Be sure thy Yillah never will be found," Joseph quoted, "or found will not avail thee."

The cat made an ugly face, crying back at him.

Chapter Sixteen

The moment Janice Hart arrived at the Meakers' on Saturday evening, she knew they were fighting. She had telephoned Maggie just one half-hour before she pulled in the drive, and Maggie had sounded quite cheerful then, but now there was a pall of tension over the place. Joseph took her coat without smiling, and Maggie made some crack about the jolly host, then, in an aside to Joseph, said, "Go on out and *drag* her in then!"

"I'm sorry to bother you," said Janice. "I didn't want to go into all of this over the phone, and I didn't think it would be right to make you come to our place."

Joseph said to Maggie, interrupting Janice. "You could at least call her! You know she doesn't answer *me*."

"Our cat," Maggie explained. "We have a new cat. It seems she prefers the outdoors to the indoors, and I don't mind saying I can see why!"

She led Janice into the living room without acknowledging Joseph's suggestion, and when they were out of his sight she made circles by her ear with her finger, then pointed the finger in the direction of the kitchen, and sighed.

Janice felt a little hurt at the fact Maggie was her old self, teasing about her husband and wisecracking with him, as though it were any ordinary evening. Maggie lit a cigarette and casually offered one to Janice, and seemed not at all eager to hear what Janice had to say.

In a whisper she said, "I've had *some* day with him! God!"

Janice thought of Lou's sad and tired eyes when he had come back from the State Police Barracks that afternoon, and she resented Maggie's petty attention to her own troubles at a time like this. Joseph Meaker, to Janice Hart's way of thinking, was a spoiled neurotic! The whole thing might not have happened if Joseph Meaker hadn't—but she stopped that thought dead in the middle. It was spilled milk. For all Maggie said about Joseph's guilty conscience, and Joseph's sensitive reacting to Lou's plight, Joseph Meaker seemed no different than usual. He had not once come to the house, not once called Louis. Now she could hear him out on the back porch shouting for the cat.

Maggie said, "I thought a new cat would make things a little better around here. Well, the cat hates Joseph and Joseph hates the cat, and everything around this place is just ducky!"

"I'm sorry, Maggie," Janice said, feeling more and more like a martyr.

"Oh, he's impossible!"

"How's the drinking?" When she said it she thought of Lou home alone. She had told him she would not be long. She had not dared hide the bottle of Jack Daniels, but she had wanted to.

"He hasn't *been* drinking today. He has the cat to occupy him!"

"It's a mess, isn't it? Look, I have something to tell you."

Behind Janice in the kitchen she could hear Joseph say, "She won't come in!"

"Then the hell with her!" Maggie shouted. Her face was very red and her hand was trembling as she knocked the ash off her cigarette.

"Go on," she said to Janice. "Never mind us."

"Lou was at the State Police Barracks all afternoon. Maggie, he decided to tell the truth, what he knows of it. He told them he was here too on Friday night, but he didn't remember it. He told them about Joseph thinking his cat had been killed by Lou, and about the book Joseph bought and gave to him, and well—the works!"

"Oh God! Really?"

"Yes. I think he was right. This is very serious, Mag. He had to tell them everything."

"Oh, Lord, I hope he didn't bring Amos Fenton into it."

"I'm afraid he did. It was Fenton he had the fight with. He *had* to bring him into it."

"Lord, oh Lord! Look, I'm not angry or anything. I just have to think."

Angry, Janice Hart thought; the hell with Amos

Fenton! She said, "I can't see what it matters! Lou's being questioned like he was a murderer! Don't you realize that?"

"Yes, honey, yes! It's just that everything is so complicated. Did they ask Lou *why* Fenton fought with him?"

"Lou told him the same thing you told us, that Fenton couldn't get him to leave, so there was a fight."

"Of course—I suppose poor Amos will be dragged into it now!"

"Well, Maggie, after all! After all! Lou's been dragged into it, hasn't he?"

"I'm sorry, honey. I'm just thinking of the newspapers."

Janice Hart felt like getting up and marching out of the Meakers', but Joseph walked into the room then and said, "Are you going to call the cat, Maggie?"

"No, Joseph, I'm not going to call the cat. The cat can sit out there on the woodpile until next May for all I care!"

"It's ominous!" said Joseph Meaker.

"Oh, the hell with it!" Maggie said. "Mix yourself a drink! Say, honey," turning to Janice now, "did you want a drink? I didn't even ask."

"I could *use* one."

"How about it, Joseph? We could all use a drink."

"The cat's one of these strange kind," Joseph said to Janice. "It's omnious, that's all."

Janice said, "Well," smiling, detesting Joseph Meaker at that moment, "I'm not very superstitious."

"Many people are, you know, particularly about cats. Welsh sailors say if the ship's cat mews constantly it portends a difficult voyage. And in some parts of France the cat was believed to be the devil and—"

"Thank you, Doctor Folk Lore!" Maggie said. "Next week the Ladies Auxiliary will present another interesting lecture entitled 'When You Entertain Guests Be Sure To See They Have A Drink In Their Hands Before You Start To Bore Them To Death!' "

Joseph walked out of the room.

While Janice talked, she could hear him rattling the ice-cube trays in the kitchen. She told Maggie of Lou's meeting with Muriel Duncan, and of Captain Plant's hammering the desk at one point and shouting at Lou that he was holding something back, and she broke down finally and wept into her handkerchief. Maggie was comforting her when Joseph finally reappeared with a trayful of drinks, and a smile.

"Our host is one up on us, I think," Maggie said, "or is it two."

"My apologies to both of you," Joseph said. "It's two. I had to calm down. I'm sorry."

"Lou met Muriel Duncan today, Joseph, at the State Police Barracks."

"I'm not really antagonistic towards that cat. I think it's the other way around." He was smiling again, pulling the hassock up to sit by Janice. "I think Yillah doesn't like me," he said.

"Joseph! This is hardly the time to talk about Yillah!"

"Nó, it's just the time. Yillah is truth, truth is Yillah!"

Janice Hart fought for control, knotting the wet handkerchief around in her palm, thinking of Lou home alone—and the bottle of Jack Daniels. He had said he was never going to drink again; they would move, he had said, when it was all over; maybe go back to Paris with Tony; a whole new environment, they would find. Throughout the ordeal, Janice had never once asked him if there were any possibility that he *did* know something about Duncan's disappearance. But last night she had dreamed of a courtroom, and Lou was on the stand, drunk. He was telling the jury he missed all the old magazines he used to read at home. Janice was sitting far in the back of the courtroom, wanting to scream at him that he was hurting his cause; didn't he realize he was on trial for his life? She had awakened trembling, grabbing hold of Lou, waking up. Just a dream, she had told him; I don't even remember it.

". . . can tell you one thing," Joseph was saying now, "this girl Muriel does not have the right kind of frames for her glasses."

"You're not funny, Joseph," Maggie snapped.

"Nor am I trying to be funny. It's the truth."

"Janice, what was she like?"

"Lou said she was very pathetic, homely, tired-looking, and tried to be very nice to him. She lost control once and begged him to tell her if he knew anything about her husband. But otherwise, she was as nice as she could be. She told Captain Plant she had never set eyes on Lou, nor heard his name before last Thursday."

"She'll probably get married again, even if she is homely. She has a square face though," Joseph said, "and the rimless glasses emphasize it. Somebody ought to tell her."

"Joseph just needs a whiff of the cork, Janice. That's all."

"I'm sorry. I'm not in the mood for jokes tonight. Anyway, Lou's home alone. I don't want to stay long." Janice put her cigarettes in her purse. "I just wanted to tell you Captain Plant will probably be around asking you questions now."

"Asking us?" said Joseph. "Why *us?*"

"Don't bother going into it again, honey. He won't remember it, anyway."

"We have nothing to hide," said Joseph. "We'll have him to dinner, this Captain Plant. How about it, Maggie?"

"Sure, sure. We'll have the whole police force to dinner." Maggie put her hand on Janice's knee. "I'm sorry, honey. I apologize for him."

"We'll have the police and Amos Fenton and the Risestaver Coffee Corporation, and T. S. Eliot and Miriam and Tom, and you can come too, Janice. Bring Louis."

He was emptying the rest of the martini pitcher as Janice stood up.

"We love the whole world," he was saying while Maggie saw Janice to the kitchen, "and you can blame it all on gin!"

At the kitchen door Maggie said, "Do you notice how he avoids any serious discussion of Lou or the entire subject?"

"Is he just drunk?"

"Drunk *or* sober he simply ignores it. Jan, I'm damn worried!"

"I'm sorry," Janice Hart said, but she was far, far sorrier for Janice Hart.

When Maggie returned to the living room she found Joseph holding up a copy of *Vogue*.

"This is what I mean," he said, "look here, Maggie."

"Look at what?"

"At this woman's face. It's square, like Muriel Duncan's. Notice the glasses this woman is wearing! These are the frames Muriel should wear. You see! They de-emphasize the squareness."

"Sit down, Joseph, and try to listen to me. Will you do that?"

"Certainly." He sat back down on the hassock, smiling, looking very interested in whatever it was she had to say.

"Joseph, you need help. Lately, you've been drinking and it's put you in a very euphoric mood, but how do you always feel the next day?"

"I have hangovers. Doesn't everybody?"

"How do you feel about your work?"

"Remember when I did my preliminary paper on the 'German Sectarians of Provincial Pennsylvania,' Maggie? Remember you said I worked too rapidly. You said I should take more time submitting my work, because it impresses people more. Remember? Well, you're right, dear."

"You're not working at all, are you?"

"Not much. No." He grinned at her.

"And what about the stuff you've been reading, Joseph? Let me see if I can remember some of the titles. *Bury the Hatchet, Blood Money, Dance with the Dead.* What about it, Joseph? You never read anything like that before."

"I don't mind that you go through my desk. You always did. You used to look for the Varda file too. I know that." He turned the empty pitcher upside down over his glass. "We'll make more, hmm?"

"All right, in a minute, if you want to. Just let's talk a bit."

"You're right, Varda was a red. She loved my soul. She had me spotted long before this! You know what she used to write to me, Maggie? She used to write, '. . . and my dear I love your soul, wise, sad, profound and exalted, like a symphony.' That's beautiful."

"Yes, Joseph, that's beautiful. What about those twenty-five-cent books?"

"Thirty-five, dear. Thirty-five cents' worth of stupidity! How stupid to make a murderer a drunk, don't you think? I *love* people when I'm drunk!"

"And when you're sober?"

"Oh, you mean all that about the cat tonight, hmm? You see, the cat doesn't like me. I don't blame her."

"Joseph, the cat hasn't had a chance to like you. You were drunk when I brought it home and you were rough with her. The next day when you were sober, you didn't pay any attention to her."

"You're wrong, Maggie. I tried to get her in. I did!"

"She's a cat, Joseph. She likes it outdoors. She was an outdoor cat."

"I realize that now. I don't mind it. She sits out there by the woodpile all the time. 'There's nothing to me and nothing to you, we all gotta do what we gotta do.' "

"You keep reciting that, Joseph. Where is it from?"

"Eliot. T. S. Eliot."

"What's it about?"

"The same thing those thirty-five-cent books are about, only it's not so low, you see? This man in Eliot's poem did a woman in. A man doing a man in isn't classic."

Maggie said, "You doing Lou Hart in, for example?"

"I never would have done in Louis, Maggie. Oh, I hated him, dear, because I thought he killed Ishmael, but I was looking for something more subtle to do Louis in with."

"And it turned out not to be so subtle. It was a fluke, wasn't it? One of those strange flukes. And now Lou is blamed for something you would have liked to do to him yourself, subconsciously."

"Say, you're good, Maggie. You ought to take it up."

"You admit it, then? All this—this suffering, Joseph, is because you feel responsible for what's happening to Lou."

"Well, let's say, I *should* feel responsible."

"You *do*, Joseph! Oh my God, it's hard to reach someone who isn't on the qui vive about psychology! You *do* feel responsible, face it!"

"Over a drink?" He got up and reached for her glass,

the same vacant grin on his face—but she was getting somewhere, wasn't she?

"Okay, over a drink."

"And then I'll propose a toast, Maggie. You know who I'm going to toast?"

Maggie felt as though she were on the precipice of a break-through, but she was not going to spoil the moment by saying Lou's name herself. Joseph had to say it.

"Do you know who I'm going to toast, Maggie?"

"Who?" She hung suspended—sure—waiting.

"Because it's Saturday night and nearly midnight," Joseph said, "I'm going to toast the other Joseph, upstairs in his study, listening to every word of our conversation!"

Chapter Seventeen

Sunday, life went on while Joseph stayed in bed. "Life" was Maggie on the telephone, and the television playing across the room from Joseph. Joseph watched two Swedish sopranos sing duets from Rossini and Dvorak, while downstairs Maggie's conversation with Amos Fenton drifted up piecemeal. There were a lot of "miGods!" and "don't worrys," and she was no sooner finished with that call than she was jiggling the tone button for the long distance operator again. Her call to Tom Spencer lasted through "U.N. In Action," and the second half of a two-part discussion on Mr. Lincoln and the Bible. Joseph caught very little of the conversation, since Maggie was practically whispering (which was anyone else's normal conversational pitch) and the cat had removed herself from the top of the television set where the speaker was, increasing the volume.

Joseph was suffering from palpitations; his heart seemed about to tear through his chest, and everytime he took his eyes off the television screen, he saw the eyes of the cat studying him. He had tossed a pillow at her just as Mark Van Doren started a poem about Lincoln. Now she was sitting on the bureau looking at him. He shut his eyes and saw her eyes there in the dark. It had been his own idea to keep the cat in all day. He knew dogs dug things up from the ground and he was taking no chances with this cat. He took a long breath, opened his eyes, and looked straight into hers.

"Get out of here!" he shouted. The cat did not even blink, and the effort cost him a clear head. The ache began by his temples and then encompassed his head like a bandeau. When Maggie shouted from downstairs, "Anything wrong up there?" he could only manage a resigned, "No."

He heard her say, "I know it's the cat bothering him," and he supposed now Tom Spencer was giving her some sage advice about what to do next. Somehow he slept through the "Bell Telephone Hour" and half of a programme called "Celebrity Golf." He had dreamed.

They were together in the same hide-a-bed she had ten or fifteen years ago when Joseph was dating her. He had told her in the dream that several days ago he had been listening to *Christ Lag in Todesbanden* and that afterwards he had killed a deer. "You would not kill a fly," she had laughed. He had run to get the fly-swatter from his kitchen to show her that he would most certainly kill a fly, but she had only laughed harder. "*Es war ein Traum*," she had told him. "It was a dream, Joseph." He had awakened at that point, and there was the cat. He imagined that the cat was smiling at him now, a lopsided, insinuating smile. When Maggie brought his supper tray, he told her he wanted the cat out of his sight. Maggie was doing everything he asked her to do today, treating him as though he were a heart case, or some sort of certifiable psychotic who would go to pieces if his coffee was over-sugared.

"Ed Sullivan," and "G. E. Theatre," "Jack Benny" and "Candid Camera." Palpitations and the headache, much worse now. At eleven o'clock he took two strong sleeping pills. It was raining out. Just as Joseph was straightening the bed sheets he heard a man's voice come over the television.

"Do you want to tell us about it, Mrs. Duncan?"

Joseph turned around and looked at the set. A slim fellow holding a microphone was kneeling by the old davenport with the antimacassars, and there was Muriel. The lights from the television camera caught the reflection of the glasses, so that her face seemed to give off sunrays, and on her lap, a child, who could be no older than two, also wore glasses, causing more sunrays.

". . . believe. So that's the way it is," she was saying.

"You don't know what to believe?"

"No." Her voice broke at that point, and she put her hand up near her glasses, while the baby in her lap pulled up her skirt. She smoothed it down and the reporter turned around in his squatting position and faced the camera. He said, "If any of you can offer any information about the whereabouts of this man, please call your local police." Then there was a gruesome likeness of Billy Duncan on the screen. Joseph walked across the room and turned off the set.

Behind him, Maggie in her nightgown said, "I suppose the police will be coming around here soon."

In the night, the rain had turned to snow. Maggie's ride tooted for her shortly after seven-thirty, and vaguely, Joseph recalled her exclaiming over the snow, over the fact the cat had been out all night. Joseph must have rolled over and gone back to sleep, for when he woke up a second time, the sun was very bright in the bed room, and there was a strange stillness, broken only by a crunching sound. Joseph sat up in bed. A car was coming down the drive, was that it? He went to the window, and then he saw them. They had pulled up outside the garage. They wore dark blue uniforms with light blue patches, caps, holsters with guns in them. *Guns?* Routine, Joseph's brain went over and over the word monotonously, routine, just routine, routine business, only routine.

The window in the bedroom was still open from the night, and Joseph knelt down under it, out of sight, listening.

"Side door," one said.

"Real crust on this stuff."

The noise of their footsteps in the snow was like strips of canvas being ripped down the middle; then there was the sound of stomping on the wooden porch. Knocking. Pounding. Joseph stood up and went and sat on the bed, pulling the robe around him.

Of course he had expected them; it was inevitable. He would only have to go down and let them in, tell them yes, Louis Hart was here the Friday before last; yes, there had been a little scuffle; yes, he had given Louis a book called *The Unknown Murderer* because he had thought Louis had killed his cat. Routine, routine; yes, to everything. Easy. He pulled the robe tighter around him, sat perfectly still. The pounding seemed more insistent.

"Tracks on the driveway, Paul. Maybe they're gone."

"Yeah."

More pounding.

"Try them tonight?"

"Yeah."

More strips of canvas being ripped, then, "Lookit!"

"Yeah. Rabbit."

"Naw, a cat! Goddam cat! Lookit it leap!"

Joseph got up and sneaked to the side of the window. He could see the men standing, facing the barn. Then he saw Yillah chasing around behind the barn. Her legs sunk down into the snow, surprising her, so that she jumped even higher. The police officers stood there chuckling.

"What is it, Paul, one of those Minx or Manx cats?"

"Siamese! Siamese—this Meaker's supposed to be some kind of cat nut."

"Siamese, huh? Looks like a rabbit. Get itself killed in small game season, bet."

"Not around here. You get a load of those signs he's got under the No Gunning ones?"

"No."

"Oh, this you got to see! Look, one on the barn. C'mon."

Joseph watched while they tramped back towards the barn. Then they stood directly under the sign Billy Duncan had stood under; one with his hands on his hips peering up at the sign through his sunglasses; the other standing beside him, shoving his hands into large gloves. For a while, they stood back there talking. Joseph watched them, his heart worse now than it had been yesterday, knocking, knocking, just the way those two had been knocking moments ago on his back door. Joseph saw Yillah again, jumping past the police, running around the barn like a crazy thing, and they were calling her. Then they went behind the barn, out of Joseph's sight.

Joseph knew a dog could dig up the hard ground, but not a cat. Not a cat! He felt perspiration break out under his pyjamas, and he was breathless now. He had no idea how much of the woodpile had been covered by the snow; and his next thought was that of a strange dog (never mind the cat) entering the yard at some point, doing exactly what Joseph was sure a cat would not do. He imagined some of the wood toppled over where the dog had started the digging; he imagined a hand. A hand sticking out of the ground. His knees felt as though they would give under him, and he held on to the sides of the bureau, and he told himself one slight giving-in to the panic could ruin him. All sorts of things occurred to him, a series of mad impulses which all logic and control made him squelch; but they were on his mind; he could stick his

155

head out of the window and shout, "I knew a man once did a man in!" He could walk calmly down, put on his overcoat over his pyjamas, go out and get in their car, then drive it straight back and into the woodpile. "Let's get to the bottom of things," he might say as he stepped out of the car. "Shovels, gentlemen?" Or—he could just begin screaming, the way he felt like screaming, just start screaming as though the top were off his head and the noise inside was let go. They were coming from around behind the barn now. Joseph studied their faces, their gaits, looking for a sign of something unusual. There was nothing. But would they show it? *They* would, Joseph thought—wouldn't they?

As they came closer, Joseph heard the man in sunglasses saying, "Yes, I hadn't thought of that."

"Anything's possible," said the other.

"Crust like I've never seen it on this stuff!"

"You ski, Paul? My kid's started this year. Up in Vermont."

Then the man with sunglasses was opening his side of the car, and the other was getting in behind the wheel.

The phone was ringing. Joseph let it ring five times, being sure the police car was well on its way down his drive before he answered it.

2

The truth was, Maggie was slipping. Tom Spencer was sorry about it, but "sorry" was not going to keep Picks Cigarettes happy with A. & F. Spencer should have known she was slipping long before this crisis in her life, but he had been a bit dazzled by old Mag, that was all. That weekend when Maggie had Miriam and him out, he had had the same feeling that client had about the commercial she had written for Picks, but he had just not been sure enough of himself to criticize it. In fact, he had gone overboard in the other direction. It was time now to stop pulling punches or playing pals-can-do-no-wrong. The client was right. A cigarette "sell" has to have power! That thing Maggie dreamed up about the whispering girl interrupting the three minutes of silence was cute, but it had no power! Worse, it was irritating, and if there was

156

one word a cigarette sell should not call to mind, "irritating" was the word.

Tom Spencer was appreciative of the fact that Maggie had her troubles, but Tom Spencer was soon going to have troubles of his own if he and Maggie did not "get with it" on the Picks campaign. After *that* got rolling, he would play all the games of Dr. Freud-what-shall-I-do-about-Joseph that Maggie wanted to play, but right now Christmas was coming and there was a small matter of a big bonus in the offing.

It was ten minutes past five now, and Maggie was on the telephone again. Spencer sat with the Picks file on his lap, waiting for her to finish. It was snowing outside, and he was half-listening to Maggie, and half-having an imaginary argument with Miriam in his mind, over the fact she had probably not done anything today about getting the snow tyres on the car.

Maggie was shouting, "What do you mean? No, don't hang up!" and Tom Spencer was giving Miriam hell in his mind, at the same time he was aware of the fact that he was displacing his anger from Maggie to Miriam.

Tom glanced down at the Picks file, and Maggie's new memos on a proposed campaign. "Picks Has A Trick In It!" Another one of her cute ideas. She had sent some secretary out to research magician's tricks, and with that material she had made up a campaign in which a magician would perform a trick, followed by an announcer saying "Picks Has A Trick Too! The trick of making truly good tobacco!" God! Anyone slightly inclined toward tongue-twisting could have the whole goddam Conley-Fast Cigarette Corporation sued for obscenity with that kind of slogan!

Maggie was holding the arm of the telephone now, staring at it dumbly.

"Finished?" said Tom Spencer sharply.

She put the telephone down and sat there. "Oh miGod."

"Listen, Mag," Spencer said, "no matter what it is, it's got to go undiscussed for a time! I've got Harrison on my neck, Mag!"

"This is something, though. This is something!"

"Maggie, goddam it, we've got about two days! Two days! This stuff about trick and Picks and Picks with a trick in it is awful! It's awful! It has no power!"

"Oh, do you sound like Harrison!"

"All right, I sound like Harrison! It's about time I sounded like Harrison! I'm getting paid by Harrison, not Freud! Not Dorothy Dix! Not Norman Vincent Peale! Maggie, goddamn it, we've both got to forget our personal lives and get with business!"

"All right. All right." But she sat back in her swivel chair as though someone had pushed her there; and Tom Spencer knew damn well her mind was as far from Picks Cigarettes as some dying cancer case's.

"The thing is," he tried, "Harrison wants power! Something that booms instead of titters, something that suggests bigness!"

"Umm, hmmm."

"Something that will make people sit up and notice, and talk!"

"How about a nice juicy scandal about Amos Fenton and me?"

Spencer hit her desk with his fist. "Maggie! Will you get off it?"

"You know, Tom, if you were a priest you'd be the kind who would announce the time of the Ladies' Sodality Bingo Game at a funeral."

Tom Spencer sank back into his chair and put his hands over his face. "I quit! I quit! I quit!"

"Sorry to hear it. Funny thing, I never thought you'd quit until after you got your Christmas bonus."

"Okay, Maggie, we won't get nasty. We won't. It's not going to get us any place, and we're not going to like each other the better for it. Okay. I'll call Miriam and tell her I'm going to be late again, and you tell me what happened on the telephone. Then maybe we can consider Mr. Harrison's wishes."

"Tom, I'm not in a mood to consider Mr. Harrison *or* his wishes. Joseph has left me!"

"He's what? Oh, my God!"

"I talked to him at noon. I called him to remind him the cat was out. He said he knew it, and he sounded perfectly okay, though he wasn't very talkative, and then I went off to lunch with Amos to try and calm him down. He thinks the newspapers are going to involve him in this Duncan case.”

“What the hell does *he* care! What the hell does goddam Amos Fenton care!”

“Oh, come *on*, Tom! Lou Hart is on a truth kick; the truth as *he* remembers it, and something just might come up about Amos and me being alone downstairs, and Joseph misinterpreting it. Oh, I’m tired. I’m just tired!”

“Well, finish the story, Maggie. What next?”

“Next? You were here when the phone rang ten minutes ago. It was Joseph. He’s in Trenton. He says he’s leaving the car there at the station for me. He says he’s not going home. ‘Where are you going?’ I asked him. ‘I don’t know,’ he said, ‘but I’m not going home again.’ I said, ‘Let me meet you and talk with you.’ And do you know what he said? He said, ‘I’m leaving you, Maggie. You’ll find someone to marry you again. Some women are too homely, but you’re not.’ ”

Tom Spencer got up and went around to Maggie’s side. “Maggie,” he said, “I’m a goddamned, pig-headed, selfish huckster! I’ll call Miriam. You spend the night with us, okay? Maggie, good Lord, I’m sorry.”

“He’s somewhere sick, Tom. That’s what keeps going through my mind. He’s somewhere sick, and I don’t think he realizes *how* sick!”

Maggie Meaker began to cry, and Tom Spencer felt as though he were watching the Rock of Gibraltar crack in half and crumble. He reached inside his coat and took out a slim cigarette case he kept next to a package of Picks.

“Pull yourself together, Maggie,” he said, offering her a Kent.

Chapter Eighteen

He left the car at the train station in Trenton, for Maggie. Then he walked to the corner and checked in at the Y.M.C.A. He asked for directions to the nearest liquor store, went out in the snow and bought a bottle, and took it up to his room. Outside in the halls Christmas carols were playing, pumped in from some central point. "Silent Night," "Jesus, Tiny Infant," along with "Rudolph, the Red-Nosed Reindeer." From the vent in his door, he could hear them. He pulled a chair over to the window, watched out, and sipped the gin from a water glass. He would never go back to the house on Old Ferry Road. He was not sure yet where he would go, but the next day, or the day after that, he would walk back down the block and get on a train. For all practical purposes, he was a man who was leaving his wife. He knew full well it would cast suspicion on him, but if he were to run, after the police interviewed him, he would look even more suspicious.

Before he had left the house he had gone out behind the barn. The wood pile was intact and snow-covered, and the cat's interest had simply been in one log, which she had been using to sharpen her claws. He had actually begun to have delusions that the cat was against him, that she was intent on exposing him to the police. Well, it was time to clear out of there, was all, before there were more delusions, before fear got a grip on him and he could no longer control the crazy impulses that had wanted to overtake him when the police were in his driveway. He had figured it out clearheaded and with considerable thought.

He had written the following note to Maggie, not unaware of the fact the police would probably be interested in its contents.

"Dear Maggie,
"In the past few weeks we've talked a lot about your suspicions that I am jealous of Amos. It is not so much jealousy (though I was surprised when Louis blurted

out that Amos was your lover, and Amos reacted by hitting him) as it is logic that leads me to this decision. "Logically, you are more suited to a man who is aggressive and strong, and who loves advertising as you do. I guess I am an eccentric of some sort, proven by my devotion to a cat, and my anger when I thought Louis ran over the cat. If I had been paying more attention to you, perhaps this whole thing between you and Amos never would have happened. Logically, it did, and I am going away, because it is the only way out for you. I expect I'll travel to New England, where I was raised, and in those serene surroundings, try to figure out what I will do next. After the holidays, I'll be in touch with you, and we can go over the practical business of separation and divorce.

"With high regards for you,
Joseph."

Maggie would not want to show that note to the police. She would not want to involve Amos Fenton. But Joseph knew Maggie well enough to be positive that she would ask Tom Spencer's opinion. Joseph knew full well how Tom Spencer felt about Fenton. "You can't withhold any information from the police, Mag," Spencer would advise, in his kindest tone, his head spinning with dreams of getting Fenton's job, once poor old Amos was removed because of the scandal.

If things got bad, they would go that way. Farther and farther away from suspicion of Joseph having any connection with Billy Duncan. Maggie would undoubtedly embellish the whole affair with her personal analysis, in the most up-to-date psychological terms, of Joseph's pitiful guilt feelings over Louis' troubles—And Louis' troubles? Joseph had read enough "thrillers" to reckon that Louis' troubles amounted to a bag of beans, so long as Billy Duncan's body remained where it was. Without a body, the Billy Duncan case had no real pulse to it. Certainly under the circumstances, the police were not going to put out a drag-net for Joseph. Tomorrow, or the next day, Joseph would head south, and stay there until the whole thing petered out.

He sat looking out the window of his room in the Y. He

161

was sad, but he knew that it was the gin, and that the sadness was a sort of lightheaded one, not heavy gloom. It was a sadness over little things. He could not remember Ishmael at all, for example, and on the drive to Trenton, he had seen hunters coming from a woods in the snow, and they had not irritated him in the least. He had only noticed that one of them was not wearing gloves, and he had thought that he was glad he had remembered to pack his own gloves. Was he without feeling? He poured more gin into the water glass. He had gone away and simply left the Varda file in his desk drawer, on top of the paperback novels. Before he had packed, he had thought of taking something from the file with him, but when he tried to pick out something he particularly liked, he could find nothing. It was like trying to find a fascinating passage in some favourite book, read when you were very young, only to discover you no longer had whatever it was you had taken to that book, and that now you could get nothing for nothing—the book was strange—you told yourself: "It didn't hold up."

He had had so many, many feelings; where were they now? He had been full of wonderful, exalted thoughts that sometimes made him soar, and now where were they? What were they, that they could go like that, with the snap of a finger, the passing of a day? Joseph leaned forward in his chair, not believing what he saw. In the distance was a church, with its glassed-in announcement board near an iron fence in the yard. He stared at the words, spotlighted in the evening. They ran in a straight line downward. They said:

CONSIDER
THOSE
AS
VICES

"Oh, no," Joseph said aloud, "not vices. They were true feelings!" He shut his eyes and drew a long breath, then opened them.

CONSIDER
THOSE
AS
VICES

"Am I mad?" He laughed, but it was because he knew
he was not mad, and there was that sign. It was nothing
from any scripture, it meant nothing, did it? Except to
Joseph, who had been asking questions of the night, from
his window there in the Trenton Y.

He decided to go out and investigate the sign. He
needed food—a hamburger, cup of coffee, and he would
walk down toward that church and try to find a lunch
stand, or a restaurant of some kind. He put on his coat,
and finished the finger of gin in his glass, then opened the
door to his room and he was flooded with a chorus singing
"Rocking Round the Christmas Tree" over the Y's public
communications speaker. Going down in the elevator he
remembered a line from La Rochefoucald's *Reflections*.
"Our virtues are most frequently but vices disguised."

Passing through the lobby, he saw a copy of a Trenton
newspaper. He stopped and flipped through it, but there
was nothing in it about Billy Duncan. On the reading
table, there were other newspapers and he walked over,
and stood there with his coat on, going through them. One
of the small-size New York dailies ran a picture of a
young man carrying a suitcase, a cross expression on his
delicate countenance. The headline said: "SON OF DR.
HART HERE FROM PARIS."

"Tony Hart, 19, son of Dr. Louis Hart whose name has
been prominent in the case of the missing war hero
from Lambertville, New Jersey, arrived from Paris last
night. Claiming that his return has nothing to do with
his father's alleged involvement in the Duncan affair,
the young artist snapped at reporters waiting at Idlewild
Airport.

"The reporters were there to greet Mindy Hill of
Hollywood fame, returning from Rome with her new
husband, Pierre Rosenbach. When it was learned that
Dr. Louis Hart's son was also aboard the Convair,
some interest was centred on the youth.

" 'My visit is a normal Christmas call on my folks,' the
boy insisted, 'and I wish you would leave me alone!'
When one reporter asked him if he thought his father
had any real connection with Billy Duncan's

disappearance, young Hart responded, 'Mind your own damn business!' Duncan, who mysteriously disappeared one week ago, left his home for a hunting trip in Bucks County. His car was found in Dr. Hart's driveway. Hart has since corrected his original story that he did not know Billy Duncan. When it was revealed that Duncan and he had a fight in a bar near Duncan's home, the Friday before Duncan's disappearance, Hart admitted that there was a possibility he met him that night. He insisted he could not remember meeting him. Police are busy with the investigation of the war hero's disappearance."

Joseph closed the newspaper and walked out of the Y. For the first time he wondered if there actually were a possibility that Louis had known Billy Duncan. He could see how stupid Billy Duncan might just park his car in Louis' drive and go off to hunt, but these reports about the fight in the Danboro Bar were an enigma. As Joseph walked along the snowy block toward the church, he played with the idea that Louis might actually have wanted to murder Billy Duncan. Perhaps he *had* known him; they had had a fight. Perhaps Louis had told Duncan to park in his drive the first day of the deer season. Louis could have gone into Tidd's Woods with a gun, and stayed there waiting for Duncan. He could have planned to kill him, then sneak back and wait until Duncan's body was found. His story could have been that he had given Duncan permission to park there, and that he supposed some hunter had killed Duncan by accident, without even knowing it. Neat and perfect. Over that weekend he had drunk for courage; he had signed the register in the motel when he was thoroughly intoxicated, his mind on only one thing: murder. Therefore, the Duncan Tondley. He may well have purposely delayed answering the Tondley call five years back, too; a murderer at heart, was all. Everything would have been all right if it had gone as Louis had planned it. More investigation went on in the case of a missing man than it did in the case of a man accidentally killed hunting. Was that the truth of the whole matter, that Louis had planned to murder Duncan And by a fluke, Duncan had wandered into Joseph's yard, and perhaps, even as Joseph was pulling the rope tightly around his neck, Louis was watching the scene from behind a tree in the woods. Joseph had committed Louis' murder for him!

This thought made Joseph's head spin. At the corner of the street he had to stop and rest his hand against a tree to support his body. Just as easily as that theory could be the truth, so could it be the truth that Louis *was* behind the wheel of his car that Sunday night the cat was killed. Who had checked on this story of the garage mechanic from New Hope?

"Oh, God!" Joseph said.

"Sir?"

Joseph looked down at a young boy with a bag of newspapers over his shoulder.

"Is anything wrong, sir?"

Joseph saw the church across the street, the bulletin board lighted up; but he had left his glasses back in the Y on the bureau. He was too far away to read the words; now he felt too weak to cross the street.

"Nothing's wrong," he told the boy, "but do me a favour, son?"

"Yessir, if I can. Are you sick?"

"No. I just wondered what that sign says in the church yard."

"The whole thing?"

"What does it say?"

"Well, it says: 'Consider those O Lord who art not with thee. Christmas Services at 10:00 a.m.'."

"Then I saw only parts of that sign," said Joseph.

"Sir?"

"Thank you. You see, I couldn't see the whole thing from my room."

"Is that all? Are you all right?"

"Yes, thank you."

So he had seen only one side of the bulletin board, and that, in parts, distorting it. Even the one clear side he *could* see was distorted. Had he also only seen one side of the whole mess he was involved in, and not even that too well? There was always too much to see, but when one saw it all put together like a jigsaw puzzle, the truth was so elementary and obvious and simple, one could feel little else but amazement that it had ever become so complex. Was that right? And if Joseph, by some magic, could see the full screen of events, summed up in some simple shot of his life, wouldn't it be of him standing there with the rope in his hand, about to strangle Billy Duncan? Billy Duncan had always been there in the shadows at his side; he knew him as well as he knew his own soul. Hadn't he always known that one day he would have to strangle Billy Duncan?

Laughter? Joseph leaned against the tree listening. He shut his eyes and suddenly he could see Louis. It was Louis laughing at him. It was Louis with a glass in his hand, toasting Joseph. "Thanks, Joe, for doing my murder for me. I told you once we were a lot alike."

"No," Joseph said in the darkness. He opened his eyes. "It was *my* murder," he whispered.

He could see his own breath in the winter's night. "Mine," he said softly.

"Mine!" Louis' voice teased in his mind. "You were just my murder tool, Joe."

Chapter Nineteen

Captain Plant put out his Cigarillo stub, grinding it into the violet-coloured ceramic leaf. "Every year," he said, "there's some nut who confesses to a crime he didn't do."

Captain McGraw, from Trenton, played with the edges of the lace antimacassar on the davenport. "It's psychological," he said.

"That's right," said Plant. "It's psychological."

Muriel Duncan was cleaning her glasses on the corner of her housedress, standing by the television, which was on, with the sound turned down. She said, "Well, I was about to die last night! I mean, holy cow, he just says, 'My name is Joseph Meaker, Muriel.' Right away he calls me by my first name, like we was first cousins. 'My name is Joseph Meaker,' he says, 'and I'm sorry to tell you I'm your husband's murderer.' Jeez!" She shook her head, and her face screwed up as though she were about to cry again. "I was—"

"Try to get a hold of yourself, Mrs. Duncan," McGraw said. "I know it's hard, at a time like this, but it's very important. Can I get you some coffee or a glass of water?"

"I'd sure like a can of beer from the refrigerator. I mean, I don't drink in the morning or anything, but this morning—"

"You don't have to apologize, Mrs. Duncan. You've been through a terrible strain. I'll get you a can of beer." McGraw got up and went to the kitchen.

Mrs. Duncan drew a deep breath, then put on her glasses in a careful way, sniffed once or twice and held her hands tightly in front of her. "You see, Captain," she said, "I just don't know whether or not I can talk to him. Do I have to talk to him?"

"We'd appreciate it very, very much."

"But if he's a nut, what does it matter what he says?"

"Mrs. Duncan, his insistence over the telephone last night that Dr. Hart had nothing to do with this, might tip us off to something about Hart we don't know. I guess you know we don't believe Hart's story."

"Yes, I do. I liked the doctor."

"He's a very personable fellow, Mrs. Duncan, but many murderers are. I'm sorry. I'm sorry to use that word. I realize it doesn't give you much hope for seeing your husband again, but I'm afraid we all have to start facing facts, Mrs. Duncan."

"Why couldn't this Meaker have done it? That's what I don't get."

"For one thing, Mrs. Duncan, he had no connection with your husband, and Dr. Hart did. For another, we were already aware of the fact Meaker was sort of an oddball. He was mad at Hart because he thought Hart killed his pet cat. Like Captain McGraw says, it's psychological. Hard to explain. We talked to Mrs. Meaker this morning at her office. She said her husband was having a nervous breakdown."

Muriel Duncan sat down in the rocking chair before the television set, twisting a wet handkerchief in her hands. "But how can you believe anything he says then?"

"Maybe we can't, Mrs. Duncan. Then again, maybe something—some one thing he says to you, will break this case wide open. Now, he says he knows where your husband's body is buried. I'm sorry, Mrs. Duncan, I have to talk this way."

She took off her glasses and wiped her eyes. "I know you do. It's all right. I says to him when he says that, 'Why don't you tell the police?' I says, and he says, 'Oh, they'll find out soon enough,' he says."

"Yes, I remember your telling me that, Mrs. Duncan. You see, he can talk to you, but not to us, I guess. That's why we're not going to just put him under arrest and take him for questioning. We don't want Meaker, Mrs. Duncan. We want Hart. And in order to get anything on him, we'll have to listen to all sorts of nuts probably. This time though, we need your help."

McGraw appeared with a can of beer for her. "I couldn't find a glass."

"No, I never use a glass. Billy taught me that. Tastes better straight out of the can. You want any?"

"No," McGraw said; and Plant shook his head. He looked at his watch. "Should be along any minute now. I'm going to dump this ashtray and get rid of my gloves

over here. Mrs. Duncan, you should act just as you would
on any morning, like you were watching TV and having a
beer.”

“I don’t drink in the morning. I don’t ever. It’s just that
this morning, I need this beer.”

“Last night he said something about the kids, didn’t he,
Mrs. Duncan?” McGraw said.

“He says probably, he says——” She was starting to cry
again.

“He said probably you’d want to remarry, because you
had all those kids, wasn’t that it?”

“Yes.”

“Yes. Well now, the idea is to get him to talk, see? He’s
got to feel easy, see? Now, he might notice the kids aren’t
around. You just tell him you sent them to your mother’s
for the day.”

“That’s the truth. I won’t get mixed-up if I tell the
truth.”

“That’s right. And there’s no need to be afraid. These
nuts who run around confessing to other people’s crimes,
they never make trouble, Mrs. Duncan. He wouldn’t make
trouble.”

“I seen some on television just scare me looking at
them.”

“Well, that’s television. This fellow is a scholar!”

“My husband used to say *I* was. I had this year at
business school. He says, ‘Well, Dr. Einstein, what’s for
supper tonight? Alphabet soup?’ ” She gave a little laugh
which exploded into a sob, and McGraw and Plant
exchanged worried looks.

Captain Plant said, “All the while he’s here, ma’am,
think of it as something you *have* to do for your husband.
Will you do that?”

“Yes. I really will. After the telephone call last night, I
says to myself, you got locks on the doors and the police
are on the way, and you’re scared, Muriel Duncan, and
here Billy went off to war and he didn’t have nothing, just
a gun with all those bombs going off. I says to myself, if
you can’t be brave once in your life, what good are you
anyway? Yes, I’ll try.”

“Anything he says about Hart, you lead him on, all
right?”

“Yes.”

“All we have to do now is wait,” Captain Plant said.

2

The snowstorm last night was a piece of luck. Maggie must have stayed in the city because of it, so that when Joseph walked to the train station that morning, he found the car still there. He had thought he might have to get a cab to Lambertville, but he went instead in his own car, and the roads were not half as bad as he had expected them to be. By now, the police were probably well ensconced in Muriel Duncan’s house, waiting for him to appear. He wondered if they would stay hidden while he talked with her, or nab him the moment he came through the door. It was the chance he had to take. He hoped they would give him time to sit there on the davenport with the white lace antimacassars, and tell Muriel Duncan quite simply how it had all come about. He had stayed awake last night trying to plan the way he would tell her, so she would understand. It was important for her to understand, just as important as it would be for Maggie to understand, if it had been Duncan who had killed Joseph.

If the police were to grab him as he stepped inside the Duncan house, well, it would be a sort of proper homecoming. Perhaps he did not deserve a chance to tell Muriel Duncan the whole story. Instead, he would have to tell the police, in some cold-feeling room, sparsely furnished, official-looking, their faces watching him as he spoke, faces that practised no show of emotion, blank, casual—“And then, Mr. Meaker? Did you bury him then?” No, he didn’t want it to be that way. He wanted to watch a real face, wanted to see it take in his words and register their meaning, wanted to see it show surprise, sympathy, the beginnings of knowledge. In a way, Joseph Meaker wanted to teach that morning, to teach by telling everything that had come to him under the tree, down from the Y, in Trenton, New Jersey.

If it went well for him (And wasn’t the car being at the station a good omen? Wasn’t the fact that the roads were clear, a good omen?) the newspapers would tell the story. How would Louis Hart feel then? Oh yes, victorious, free,

170

but perhaps slightly let down too? It was all Joseph's murder, like the legendary bullet that hit the certain soldier of war, Joseph's name was on this murder. He had been going in the direction of it all his life. He had been neither tricked into it, nor had he stumbled into it; it may as well have been meticulously planned for all the years he could reason. There was a certain sadness attached to the fact he had not always recognized that person beside him in the shadows, but how many people in life at least saw once, face to face, their shadow partner, and grappled with him? Not Louis, certainly—Louis had ahead of him years of misery; well, didn't most people? Joseph's life was complete; it had gone a full circle exactly. Wasn't there a beauty in that? For most people, life was going around and around in circles. Joseph had read a poem once about that; he remembered that it ended: ". . . and the secret sits in the middle and knows."

At the white wooden bungalow on Landers Lane in Lambertville, Joseph pulled the Consul to the kerb. Not a sign of a police car anywhere. He smiled. Were they inside behind the curtains with drawn guns? He got out, straightened his tie, and walked up the winding slate-stone path. There was a pink wooden crane stuck into the ground near bushes by the doorstep. Joseph shook his head. Well, that was what he had been spared in life—pink wooden cranes; one never saw the decor in one's shadows, that was something to be thankful for!

He punched the bell three times fast, then waited for this woman who could well have been his wife, had fate pushed him a little this way, a little that.

She appeared then behind the storm door, her glasses mixing in with the glint from the glass windows which the noon sun struck.

"I'm Joseph Meaker," he said when she opened the storm door.

"Come in."

He wiped off his feet on the doormat, which had a green turtle woven into it. He was spared a green turtle as well as a pink crane; there were many things to be thankful for, yes. He was spared many, many things. A tin umbrella stand painted gold with FOR A RAINY DAY embossed across it; a china duck with a cactus plant for a tail; *Reader's Digest* on the end table on top of a copy of the official *American Legion Magazine*; a large black satin pillow with gold tassels hanging off it, CAMP CROWDER embroidered on it in orange; and then—then the antimacassars. He sat down on the davenport.

"Antimacassars," he said. "Do you know why they're called that, Muriel?"

She was turning off the television set. ("Keep your television set on," the police must have said, "make believe it's like any other day.") She did not look him in the eye, but kept her eyes down on the rug. Spared: one rug, brown and gold, with kittens tangled in yarn woven into the pattern.

"They're called antimacassars because men used to wear an oily hair tonic called Macassar. It left stains on the furniture. Thus, antimacassar." He smiled at her, but she turned her eyes away from his, and sat in the rocking chair twisting her handkerchief.

So he was not going to be nabbed right away! Good!

"Muriel," he said, "I'm very much like your husband. You don't realize that, do you?"

"No." Barely a whisper.

"No. I didn't realize it for the longest time myself. A lifetime, as a matter of fact. A lifetime. Oh, you should have known me only a few months ago, before I knew myself. I was a very tense person. People thought I was shy, reclusive, do you understand? I was very tense. My wife used to say I was always holding myself in."

"Did you come here to tell me that?" Joseph wished she would not be so nervous, twisting that handkerchief in knots. He wished he could make her feel at ease.

He said, "No. I came here to tell you that Louis Hart is innocent."

"How do you know Dr. Hart is innocent?" She was barely able to talk. Joseph felt sorry for her. Those glasses would never do either. She would have to pull herself together, if she were to marry again.

"I told you last night. *I* murdered your husband." He saw her tighten up, her back went rigid, and the veins in her arms stood out as she clenched her hands together. "Muriel, listen, in a way Billy and I were brothers! He was the same kind I was! Was, I mean I'm not—"

She interrupted him. "What about Louis Hart? Dr. Hart?"

"Him! He wanted to murder your husband, I think. I'm not sure, but I think he did. I didn't think so until last night. Last night everything was very clear to me. Did you ever have a moment of absolute lucidity, Muriel? When everything was clear?"

But she was simply not interested. That was the crazy part; she was simply not interested in what Joseph had to say.

She said, "Why would Louis Hart want to kill my husband?"

"They had a fight in Danboro, didn't they?"

"Do you know about it?"

"Muriel, *I'm* the murderer, not Louis Hart. Aren't you interested in *me*?"

"I just wondered what the fight was about? Between Dr. Hart and Billy?"

"Oh, God knows, Muriel, what *that* was about! Probably more of Louis' theories about this and that! I think he told Billy to park his car out in the patients' parking lot, that's the way I see it. As I reconstruct it, Billy was worried about this pheasant he lost, you see? And he wanted a safe place to park his car."

Muriel Duncan said, "How did *you* know about the pheasant?"

"I took it from his car."

"I remember now," said Muriel Duncan. "He told me someone took his pheasant! I remember him saying that Saturday morning. He says, 'Someone stole my pheasant, Mure. Someone stole my pheasant.' "

"Sure," Joseph smiled. "That was me."

"You took his pheasant?"

"Sure. And I murdered him Monday morning, Muriel. I suppose Louis is getting credit for taking the pheasant too. No, that was me. Billy's buried right by that pheasant, Muriel. I buried him with his deer—" but Muriel was weeping now, very loudly, her head down in her hands. Joseph got up off the davenport to go across to her, and then the policemen appeared.

Joseph said, "Good morning, Officers."

"Good morning, Meaker," one said. A New Jersey
173

policeman. The other was from Pennsylvania.

Muriel was being led from the room by the New Jersey policeman. "I remember about the pheasant now," she was crying. "Billy said, 'Mure, someone stole my pheasant!' " The New Jersey policeman was calming her, and the other policeman was taking some cellophane off a Cigarillo.

He said to Joseph, "I'm Captain Plant from Doylestown."

"How do you do?"

"You don't seem very surprised, Meaker."

"I knew you were there."

"So you're Billy Duncan's murderer, hmmm?"

"Yes. He's under the woodpile, out behind my house."

"Uh-huh. Sure, Meaker." Captain Plant smiled pleasantly, sucked on his Cigarillo and regarded Joseph with an amused expression.

Joseph shook his head sadly. "Captain, do you think I'm out of my mind?"

"Do you think you are, Meaker?"

"Not out of it, *in* it, in a sense. *In* it, for the first time!"

"Well, Meaker, you can come along with us and we'll have a long chat about it."

"All right."

"McGraw, I'll wait out in the car with him. I'll bring it around out front."

McGraw walked back into the room. "Why don't you take him in? I'll stay here with her until we get someone else over here. She's afraid, I think. Is someone picking up Hart?"

"Yes." Captain Plant knocked an ash from his Cigarillo into a plastic ashtray, shaped like a top hat.

"What has Louis got to do with this any more?" said Joseph. "You mean she's still afraid of Louis?"

The police officers ignored him. They were talking together now, leaving him to stand there in the middle of the living room, unguarded.

Joseph could see into the kitchen. Spared: a red cupid with wrapping string coming out of his bow. Muriel was standing there with her back to the doorway.

"I'll call from here to say I'm bringing Meaker in," Captain Plant said.

McGraw said, "Yeah, okay."

"Use your phone, Mrs. Duncan?"

Muriel turned around then. "Yes," she said, "go ahead."

She was holding her glasses in her hand, starting to put them on.

"Wait!" Joseph said. He started to rush across to her, but McGraw stopped him, held him by the arm.

"I only wanted to tell her about her glasses," said Joseph.

"Okay, Meaker, let's go out to the car and wait for Captain Plant."

Joseph said, "Muriel, you'll probably want to marry again. If you had heavy frames it would detract from the squareness of your face. Those rimless glasses make your face look too broad. I saw a picture in *Vogue* of—" but Muriel Duncan was screaming now, screaming hysterically, and McGraw was pulling Joseph across the living room towards the door.

On the telephone Captain Plant was chuckling. "Oh sure, it's an air-tight confession, Paul. Body's out behind his barn under the woodpile. Sure," chuckling again, "with a deer and a pheasant. *You* heard me—ha! ha!"

Joseph stumbled into the tin umbrella stand. Then he stood up, and McGraw let go of him. "Let's wait out in the car, Meaker, okay?"

"I just wanted to tell her about her glasses," Joseph said.

McGraw had a smile on his face. "You can tell her about her glasses some other time, fella."

He opened the door, and they went down the slate walk, past the pink wooden crane and away from Muriel and the white bungalow.

"No one believes me, do they?" Joseph asked.

"Let's just say you're going to put people to a lot of trouble, Mr. Meaker. You don't really want everyone digging up your yard, do you?"

"No, but they have to find the body."

"Car's around the corner," McGraw sighed. "Keys in yours?"

"Yes."

"Someone will bring yours in later."

The sun was melting last night's snow. There were several small children digging in a drift with tin shovels. They did not even look up as Joseph walked by with McGraw. It seemed like any other perfectly ordinary December day. Where were the handcuffs? The police sirens? The hostile knots of neighbours with their naked curiosity, staring at Joseph?

McGraw's voice was calm and nearly solicitous. "We had a talk with your wife this morning."

"With Maggie?"

"She's worried about you, Meaker. She sounds like she understands you pretty well."

"Oh yes, yes," Joseph sighed. "Everyone understands me."

"We only think people don't understand us," said McGraw.

And what about the other Josephs? How many of them right at that moment were walking down streets like Landers Lane in Lambertville, New Jersey, sunny winter day near Christmas, looking like anyone else, knowing what they knew—listening to policemen tell them they were understood—waiting for recognition, of any kind—of *any* kind?

"I'll say one thing," McGraw drawled out as they reached the corner, "You were right about Mrs. Duncan's glasses. Heavy frames would suit her better."

Well, that was recognition of a kind. The rest would come slowly, the way it does to the Josephs of the world.

www.ingramcontent.com/pod-product-compliance
Lightning Source LLC
Chambersburg PA
CBHW010639100726
47900CB00011B/2897